THE QUIZ

2nd Edition

WESSAM ELDEIN

It is never the number of years that counts, but it is always what you accomplish during those years. Thank you, our friend, brother, and mentor, for being part of our family and for the significant impact, touching the lives of many other families; all of us—especially the kids—cherished and remarkable memories with many stories to tell!

Your knowledge, manners, and ethics will continue as a heuristic process; you are an everlasting role model for everyone who crosses paths with you.

Thank You for the unforgettable time you spent with us in this life.

RIP Michael DiQuinzio, "The Quiz."

Table of Contents

The End

Los Angeles - California

Monday, March 19, 2035

10:10 pm

My name is John Carter. Ten minutes ago, I was one of the oldest humans living on Earth. I will… BANG….

John stopped typing when he heard a gunshot coming from the apartment next to him.

"That must be Peter," John whispered.

At the exact moment, a message appeared on his phone, laptop, and TV.

"John Carter, congratulations, you made it. You are officially one of the oldest humans living on Earth. We grant you free and endless resources starting now; enjoy!"

The message faded; John looked back to his computer, and before he started typing again, his doorbell rang!

The closed-circuit TV showed his front door; a drone had dropped a bag.

"Here is my favorite coffee, sandwich, and …. a gun."

He held the gun closer to his face, looking at his reflection in a mirror next to his desk; he paused for a second, looking at himself in his black robe that matched his salt and pepper hair and beard, placing the gun aside and fixed his reading glasses, looked back at his computer, he begins to type again…

"My name is John Carter. Today, I am officially one of the oldest humans living on earth. I will enjoy this title for the next 24 hours before I kill myself. Today, I am 40 years old!"

Terry

Brooklyn – New York

Monday, March 3rd, 2025

Time 5:30 am

Ring!

John snoozed his alarm and mumbled in an exhausted voice, "Another day in paradise!"

With a sudden burst of energy, he jumped off the bed to start his day with fifty pushups as a wake-up routine.

He went to the bathroom, and pinned on the mirror was a note that said…

"You are awesome…Go, prove it to the world."

John read the note aloud, smiled, and said, "Yes…I will."

My name is John Carter, and I am 29 years old, about to turn 30 in a few days. I am tall, good-looking, and athletic, with thick black hair, a baby face, and a nice short beard that helps me look older. I am a reporter at "Facts," a popular weekly newspaper in New York, one of the few newspapers that is, in fact, still printing, although almost everything is digitalized.

My role model and superhero is Clark Kent, aka "Superman"; his character was the reason I pursued this career. However, my life's thrill level is nothing compared to Clark Kent…yet!

Like many dreamers, I felt that someday I would engage with something to change and protect the world, but I never knew that the someday would be today!

John looked at himself in the mirror. He wiped his glasses that he didn't need but wore anyway because they made him look like Clark Kent.

With quick steps, John left the building holding his coffee, heading toward the subway.

"Good morning, John," Laura said.

"Hey, good morning, Laura. Happy Monday," John said. "I called you yesterday to play chess."

"Oh... yeah, sorry, I had girls' night; how about tonight?"

With a sly smile, John replied, "I don't see a reason why not. Remember, before I say goodnight, I always say…checkmate!"

"You wish. We'll see, silly!"

Laura Midgley had been my neighbor for many years. In her late thirties, white, tall, blonde, and skinny, Laura is a psychiatrist and has been a family friend for several years. We play chess almost every night. I win nearly every night!

John and Laura waved before they both disappeared into the crowd.

"Good morning, Peter!"

Peter was a receptionist at Facts newspaper. He is the first face you see in the morning and the last face you see at night. No matter how early I go or how late I leave, he is always there. Peter is in his late twenties, constantly smiling whether he tells you good or bad news.

Peter said smiling, "Good morning, John, the boss is here waiting for you!"

"Yep, another day in Paradise," John mumbled while walking to the chief editor's office.

"Good morning, Mr. Jackson." Mr. Jackson (Terry) could feel the energy in John's greeting.

"Good morning, John, be seated." Terry Jackson is our Chief Editor and is in his late forties; he is African American, has curly hair, and wears thick glasses with a big black frame that always slides on his nose. He is tall, muscular, and has a big gray mustache. Terry loves his job more than anything else. He is always the first to be at the office and the last to leave, not counting Peter. He is always loud, excited, and screaming all the time, but he is very supportive... Terry is a genuine and transparent soul; even his office walls are all glass.

John: "Are you doing okay, Terry? You look exhausted!"

Terry ignored John's comment and, in a calm voice, replied, "Your report about this Virus is upsetting many people."

"That means a lot of people are reading the paper!" John sounded proudly happy.

With his eyes still on the papers and a subtle smile, Terry replied, "Yes, our numbers are through the roof this week. However, I think you are exaggerating about this conspiracy theory!"

John looked like a professor about to start a lecture. "Terry, I am pretty sure this virus issue is just an economic war and overwhelming propaganda started by China so they can control the global financial market!"

Terry interrupted him, "As if they need all that to control a market they already control. Wasn't that the same debate five years ago when we all blamed China for the Coronavirus?!"

John continued like he hadn't heard Terry, "There are many facts to support my theory. First, they arrested the doctor who discovered

Terry Interrupted him again, "Tonight, John…. your flight is tonight. You will find the tickets and all other information with Peter."

Terry looked back at the papers on his desk and continued, "This is a bag of Suzan's favorite coffee; please tell her I said Hi!"

John was about to say something but held his thought, turned, and left the office.

If John had looked back at Terry's office, he would see Terry holding the phone, saying, "All good…. he's leaving tonight."

On his way back to the subway, John passed by the coffeehouse next to the newspaper building, where he usually takes lunch every day. Sometimes, he meets Laura and has Lunch with her, but today, he decided to skip lunch as he was running late!

Through the coffee shop window, he saw the waiter, chubby, short, almost bald. He looks smart with his sharp eyes and pointy long nose.

They waved at each other and smiled.

The manager standing by the door waved to John as a signal to come inside.

John waved back, "Sorry, not today."

On his way back, John kept looking at the coffee bag, repeating Terry's words, "Suzan's favorite coffee."

He prepared his luggage and then left for the airport. He couldn't stop thinking about his meeting with Terry; something was wrong, especially how abruptly Terry had ended the meeting!

Terry was not just his boss; he was also Suzan's ex-husband. After they agreed to divorce five years ago, Suzan decided to move to Los Angeles with their only son. Terry and Suzan have been married for over ten years, and Terry knows very well that Suzan …doesn't drink coffee.

Suzan

Los Angeles - California

Tuesday, March 4th, 2025

Time 2:00 am

"Ladies and Gentlemen, welcome to Los Angeles." The pilot announced.

John woke up as the plane landed. He picked up his rental car from the airport and drove straight to the hotel, rested for a little while before he started the day with his daily routine: a workout followed by a shower; he didn't forget to write his quote on the bathroom mirror, "You are awesome…Go, prove it to the whole world!"

It was already 7:00 am, so he decided to give Suzan a good morning call.

"John!! Good morning… a long time. Is everything okay?"

"Yes, all good…. I am here in LA. Are you home today or busy?"

Suzan was surprised, "Oh, you're here! We are at home today; Joseph is sick and skipped school today; you can stop by anytime."

"OK, let's all have breakfast together."

Suzan Garner, My half-sister. A virologist, almost forty. When you look at Suzan, it's almost like you are looking at a Hollywood star celebrity. She is tall, has long black hair with a round face, wide eyes, a small nose, a light-skinned athlete body, a soft voice, and a very strong personality; super smart. After the divorce, she decided to focus on her career and her son…

"You are getting bigger and stronger, Joseph."

Joseph started laughing, followed by hard coughing, "Thanks, Uncle John!"

Joseph, my nephew. Ten years old. Joseph is like an exact copy of me. We both share the same dark hair and the same baby face. He is a super-intelligent kid and loves to read, especially history. When Joseph was born, he showed signs of Autism. Suzan worked with him daily, embracing all the gifts that came with his case. He is super good at solving puzzles, and he mastered chess in record time, to the point where he could even beat me. Terry was engrossed in his career and didn't give enough time to his family. That was why they ended up getting a divorce. Joseph is now dealing with people but with certain limits. He is more of an introvert; he can easily spend hours reading history, especially Egyptology!

"Welcome to Los Angeles." Suzan greeted John while standing at the front door.

John carried Joseph on his back and walked to Suzan to hug her. "How is my gorgeous sister doing?"

"I've had some crazy days, John. Breakfast is ready." Suzan replied.

Inside the house, they all sat around the kitchen table. Joseph sat at the end of the table and started reading a History Book.

John looked at him with a warm smile before speaking to Suzan, "I guess loving history runs in the family."

"This is from Terry."

He handed the coffee bag to Suzan, waiting for her reaction.

Suzan looked at the coffee bag and put it aside, paused for a second before she looked up at John and stuttered, "How is New York and how is..." she paused again before continuing, "How is Laura doing?"

John looked at her, surprised by her reaction, "All good, same as always, Laura is fine. I wish you guys would reconnect and talk like you used to."

Suzan immediately changed the subject. "I liked your fiction report about the ongoing Coronavirus; I think you are underestimating this virus. You could use some scientific sources on this report, a virologist, for example," she said, pointing to herself.

"You sound like Terry."

Suzan replied with a smile that faded quickly. "I married him for a reason."

John continued, "He also thinks the report was more about a conspiracy theory, and it underestimates some facts about the virus; I was planning on using you as a validated source on the second part of the report. However, I still believe it is like any other flu; it is different but not as dangerous as the media portrays it to be..."

Joseph interrupted them with another hard cough stronger than the first one.

Suzan ran and brought a glass of water to him while John looked at Joseph and started to worry before he asked Suzan in a concerned voice, "Do you think he has the virus?"

"No, I already had him tested. This one is a regular flu. Anyway, why are you getting panicked? I thought you said this virus is just like any other flu."

Suzan looked straight into John's eyes before she continued, "John, this virus is not like a regular flu. This virus is not like anything we've seen before. Not even like the one we had five years ago." Suzan seemed more serious now.

"What do you mean?" John started to get worried.

She continued, "There are two different kinds of viruses. A virus that spreads rapidly but isn't deadly dangerous like regular flu. And a virus that is deadly but spreads slowly like the SARS in 2003."

John asked with full attention, "And this virus, which kind?"

She paused for a second and then spoke softly, "BOTH."

She continued, "It is a deadly virus that spreads rapidly. For example, SARS spread over 8000 cases worldwide and killed 800 people; it had a 10% mortality rate, compared to this new Virus, with a mortality rate of 3.5%. You would think it is not that dangerous, but you realize that this virus spread over a hundred thousand so far, and almost 3500 of them died. Now you see things differently."

She looked at him and continued, "In 2020, we faced coronavirus that spread rapidly and deadly, but it was easy to notice its symptoms, and it took time before it controlled the body! But that was just the beginning, like the first level of a video game or the tip of an iceberg. The real challenge is what we are facing now."

John ignored her voice and tried to defend his point; "Yes, but way more people die every year from smoking, cancer, car accidents, and…"

Suzan seemed irritated, "And what, John? And what! Just because people are dying from all these causes, it is okay to have another killer on the table?!"

John felt his sister's anger and tried to calm her down. "No, of course not."

Suzan, still angry, continued, "We are working on different treatment techniques to cure cancer. We try to make roads safer to avoid car accidents. We keep trying to control smoking and keep the air clean. We are trying to see a light at the end of the tunnel. There are different organizations with different budgets and dedicated workforces to handle each issue, but with this virus, we are in a race with something we have no clue about. In addition, only one organization must find the solution with a limited workforce and limited budget, adding to that working on other healthcare issues. This is the problem, John. We don't have control. We don't have enough information. We don't have enough workforce. We are getting tired. We are getting exhausted! We're like someone trapped in the backseat of a car heading to a cliff!"

Suzan started crying, her whole body shaking.

John rushed to hug her. "I don't know why we didn't have this conversation before I wrote this report!"

"Because you are my impulsive little brother." John felt the humor in her tone.

"Is that just a nice way of calling me stupid?"

"You can say so," Suzan laughed.

Joseph looked at us calmly, waiting to see how the conversation would end. He saw his mom laughing; he smiled and got back to reading.

Suzan wiped her tears and returned to her calm and professional voice, "The way this virus is spreading and acting is different; it looks like it is…"

She stopped saying anything further.

John wondered, "It's what?"

"I don't know, John, it's unlike anything I've seen before. All the tests, measures, and studies of this Virus point to a primitive virus that couldn't survive for a few minutes outside the host. This virus is mutating. It can survive for days outside the host. It keeps changing its behavior as if it's thinking and adapting!"

John was confused, "Thinking and adapting?"

Suzan explained, "It is like coronavirus in size, but it keeps mutating and enhancing its behavior, as for now it could survive more. It could stay hiding for more days before symptoms even start, and now symptoms aren't clear; with more and more symptoms added, it has started infecting other parts besides the lungs. We've started noticing heart-related issues, John; it's not just the flu. Regardless of how it started and who benefits from it, this virus differs from anything we knew before. I am working on something and will let you know when I have the best possible results."

The way she said she was working on something sounded strange, and John worried for his sister, "Suzan, something doesn't sound right; you know you can talk to me."

Suzan took a deep breath and looked at him. She calmly spoke after a moment, "Right after the divorce, I received a job opportunity to move here to Los Angeles, but the email I received was titled quid pro quo."

Confused, Suzan continued, "The one who sent this email said he would help me to get a great job vacancy in Los Angeles, but I need to help them on a project without asking questions."

John looked at her in surprise and said, "What did you get yourself into?"

"Nothing, it is just research about DNA transformation. I didn't even understand the point of the research, but as soon as I did the task, I got the job offer. John, I needed this job to move on."

Suzan looked away for a second and asked, "So, what brings you to Los Angeles?"

"Terry asked me to cover a Pharaoh exhibit at California Science Center."

"Which Pharaoh... King Tut?"

Joseph's eyes opened wide with excitement as he intervened, "No, Mom, not just the King Tut exhibit; this is about the 18th Dynasty in ancient Egypt focusing on Amenhotep the Fourth and his son-in-law King Tutankhamun."

"Wow, Joseph, I am impressed; you know about Amenhotep the fourth?" John was genuinely and pleasantly surprised.

"Yes, Uncle John! I like reading about this era. Did you know he changed his name to Akhenaten?" Joseph smiled.

John was admiring his nephew. "Joseph, I will need your help on this report, and let's start this report by interviewing you."

He picked a paper from the table and rolled it as a mic. Then, he changed his position facing Joseph and asked in a serious tone, "What do you think was the main reason that made pharaohs build this amazing civilization?"

"I think…." He paused and looked to the ceiling as he tried to find the right words before he looked back. "I think they were challenging their minds."

"What do you mean challenging their minds?"

"I mean, they always believed everything is possible, then turned beliefs into actions, like they believed in the afterlife, so they looked for the right tools, like mummification, to preserve the body to be ready to meet the soul in the afterlife."

John was intently listening.

"It is a tactic, Uncle John, and they mastered this tactic, always challenge the mind, to reach the goal, and that is what Akhenaten did; he challenged all the taboos."

John looked at Joseph proudly and said, "I will need your help, Joseph. Would you like to join me when I go to the museum?"

Joseph jumped off the chair, hugging his uncle. He then looked toward his mom as if seeking permission. Suzan nodded in approval, and Joseph responded with a huge smile of joy and appreciation.

John looked at Suzan, "Would you like to join us?"

"Oh no. You guys have fun, and I will spend tomorrow doing some research. Then we can all meet later. Why don't you stay here with us during your visit, John? Joseph would be so happy; I miss spending time with my younger brother."

"Yes, Uncle John! Please stay!"

John looked at them and said, "OK, I will check out from the hotel and stay with you starting tomorrow."

Joseph

Los Angeles - California

Wednesday March 5th, 2025

Time 9:00 am

It was a typical Los Angeles Sunny day when Joseph and I walked into the California Science Center. Joseph was so excited, checking the map and pointing to the Egyptian hall where the exhibit was located. Since we started driving, he hadn't stopped talking about the exhibit and the ancient Egyptian Pharaohs.

Joseph, really excited, said, "Egyptian history is overwhelming. No matter how much you dig into it, it's just a drop in the ocean."

"Did you know Cleopatra ruled Egypt around 52 BC? That's exactly 2072 years ago; however, the Pyramids were built around 2500 BC. Do you see what that means?!"

"Joseph, how could you keep track of all these dates? And what does that mean?"

"It means when Cleopatra ruled Egypt, the pyramids were already created 2450 years ago! Now, how amazing that is!"

"Cleopatra is closer to us time-wise more than she was closer to the Pyramids' era, and that means during her time, she was looking at the Pyramids era, like how we are looking at the era of ancient philosophers like Socrates and Aristotle now, or like how we look at the era of Alexander the Great."

"Isn't that overwhelming when thinking of History? I picture an old man with a long white beard writing in his big book about all the world's stories, but this man was once a kid born and grew up in Egypt."

John was speechless at how his nephew was really into history and how he expressed his thoughts.

"One day, this old man will write in his book pages and pages about you, Joseph, and…"

Joseph interrupted him and pointed at the Egyptian Hall, "We are here."

Joseph scanned all the statues until his eyes stopped at one corner. He ran to this corner and stood there without saying a word.

John asked, "What is the difference between this statue and the others?"

"This is Amenhotep the fourth or Akhenaten."

John nodded and said, "He looks different, unlike the other statues."

Joseph felt proud because he knew how to address his uncle's concern. "That is how they want him to look like. During his time, and after he was married to Nefertiti, he abandoned the traditional Egyptian Polytheism because they worshiped multiple gods, but he decided to follow one God called 'Aten,' represented by the sun. Replacing Amun, the Egyptians' greatest god at that time was represented by the moon. That is why he changed his name, then moved to a different city and built other temples that looked different from that time's usual temple designs. That upset the priests of Amun's temple. After he died, they tried to wipe out all his memories and make his statues look ugly so that people would lose respect for him and for his religion. Even his son-in-law and successor changed his name to follow the Amun Traditions."

"Joseph, I am so proud of you. You already gave me a great introduction to my report. So, by son-in-law, you mean King Tut?"

"It is not confirmed if King Tutankhamun was his son or son-in-law. King Tut's statue is over there at that corner, and Akhenaten's wife, Nefertiti, is that beautiful, colorful statue here. She is full of secrets!" Joseph pointed his finger toward Nefertiti's statue.

"Why?"

Joseph walked to the Statue of Nefertiti and stood still while looking at the queen before he answered his uncle, "She was not from a royal family or related to any priests. She was a normal girl, and for a pharaoh to marry a regular girl was odd and unacceptable. But he loved her so much, and all his statues and graffiti show their love story and how strongly he felt for and was attached to her. They got married not long after, and he abandoned his beliefs. He changed his name and moved from the capital, Thebes, to Tell El-Amarna. No one is sure if that was a coincidence or if Nefertiti was behind all that."

"What do you think?" The voice came from behind.

John and Joseph turned to look, and both paused at what they saw. Their eyes got wide open.

In front of them was standing The Queen Nefertiti!

Sarah

John stopped typing when a smile found its way to his lips as he remembered that day when he saw Sarah for the first time.

She was like a princess straight out of a history book, a queen from the ancient Egyptian era—who decided to jump thousands of years to meet them face to face. Both John and Joseph felt the same way about her…astonished!

Her name was Sarah Adam. That was how she introduced herself in her deep, beautiful voice that made John feel hypnotized.

Sarah was a living copy of the statue of Nefertiti. Everything, especially the eyes; eyes that made you feel lost and wish you never come back.

John sighed before he got back to the screen and continued typing.

***

Sarah broke the silence by introducing herself.

"I am sorry to have interrupted your conversation. I am Sarah, Sarah Adam." Her voice was as soothing as her smile.

John, still mesmerized by her eyes, said, "Hi. No, of course, you didn't! I am John, and this is my nephew, Joseph!"

Unlike Joseph's custom when dealing with strangers, he surprisingly extended his hand and said, "Nice meeting you, Sarah!"

Sarah smiled. "Nice meeting you as well, Joseph. I love your name. It's a common name in my home country, Egypt, and it's Arabic. "It means Youssef."

"Thank you. I like your name too."

"You're from Egypt; no wonder you look like her." He said that while pointing to Nefertiti's statue."

Sarah laughed aloud. "Oh, Thank you. Do you think I look like her? I'm flattered."

John tried to get into the conversation, "Joseph, I think Sarah is prettier than Nefertiti."

Sarah looked at him with a smile that melted his heart. "Thank you, John. I see from where Joseph got his speaking skills."

John was encouraged by her smile and her compliment, "So, Sarah, you're from Egypt? Do you live here in Los Angeles?"

Still looking into his eyes and smiling, Sarah said, "No, I am an Egyptologist, and I am here with the crew accompanying the exhibit. When it's done, I will be heading back to Egypt."

"Egyptologist, and your last name is Adam; that explains a lot!"

Sarah looked perplexed and paused.

John lost his voice for a second and got nervous trying to explain the joke. "I mean Adam and ancient Egyptian history and…"

Sarah interrupted him with her amazing laughter, "You should see your face; I got the joke…silly!"

"Speaking of the last name, what is yours, John?"

"Sorry, I didn't introduce myself properly. John Carter!"

Sarah smiled. "Oh, Carter, and you are here at the 18th dynasty Exhibit."

John looked puzzled!

"Are you related to Howard Carter, who discovered King Tut's mummy?"

John smiled and answered quickly, "No, I wish!"

Sarah smiled at him before looking at Joseph. She continued, "I am sorry I interrupted your conversation, but I was amazed by your information about history, especially the era of the 18th dynasty!"

Joseph nodded with a friendly smile. "Thank you."

John tried to get the conversation back. "Sarah, I am a reporter at Facts newspaper and am working on a report about the exhibit. Could you be my source on this report?"

"I would need to check with my boss, Dr. Jacob. But I don't think it should be a problem. But for now, I can be your tour guide; how about that, Joseph?"

Joseph smiled and nodded.

"This is your lucky day, Joseph," John said with a smile.

Sarah walked in front of them, leading them through the big hall.

As they followed her, they didn't see the smile on Sarah's face; it wasn't that same charming smile now. It was different, more like…mysterious!

David

Suzan walked to her office with a million thoughts in her mind that morning. She didn't even notice her colleague, Dr. David Lee, waving at her!

David Lee, an Asian American virologist, was born and raised in Los Angeles. He spoke Mandarin fluently as his first language, besides his English flow. He and Suzan are close friends. They worked together on many projects, building a solid team and friendship.

"Hey, Suzan, you didn't see me waving to you when you came in?"

"Oh, David, I'm sorry, my mind must've been elsewhere."

"Meet me in the lab. There is something you need to see!" David said in a voice that sounded like caution.

"What is going on, David? You sound serious?!"

They walked to the lab. David looked around to make sure no one else was in the lab.

"Suzan, what I'm about to tell you is confidential—a secret. No one else can know until we complete this research."

Suzan was now getting nervous.

"You know that the virus usually starts in the throat and stays there for up to four days before starting to attack the lungs, and during all this time, we were studying the nature of this virus and drawing flowcharts of its behavior, but we overlooked an important point!"

"What Point?"

"We all assumed this virus is from the same family that hit us in 2019… Remember?"

"Yes, but this is not an assumption; this virus follows the same behavior. Besides, we can see it under the microscope and…"

"Yes, we see it under the microscope when it is already infecting the body, but not before." David Interrupted

"David, how will we identify it in the body before it gets infected?"

"I don't think infected is the right term; it is more like… invaded!"

Suzan's eyes opened wider, but she couldn't speak.

David took a deep breath and continued, "Last week, I took a few experimental Rats to my house; one of them was infected by the virus, and I also took the electron microscope."

Suzan gasped. "What. You did what? Are you crazy? You could easily lose your job, and even worse, you could go to jail; you took an infected rat out of the lab to an unsecured facility, and the electron microscope that you know is not allowed to leave the building. What were you thinking?"

David looked at her before he spoke in a calm voice, "Are you finished? Because I am not finished yet, and I can't if you keep interrupting me like that."

Suzan looked at him and said, "I don't want to be a part of this; I am not ready to lose my job or face charges." She turned and moved towards the door, but something made her stop and go back, 'Curiosity!' She walked back to him and said, "OK, I'm listening; please make it quick."

David smiled and continued, "OK, So I injected a Nano-chip camera in the throat of the five healthy rats and the one that was infected by the virus. Then I connected all the cameras with the electron microscope, put one of the healthy rats with the infected one, and started monitoring the cameras on both. As soon as the rats got closer to each other, I saw the virus showing up in the healthy rat's throat."

"OK…This is expected; the other rat gets infected…I mean invaded, as you call it," Suzan interrupted again.

David stopped talking and gave her a look.

"OK, Sorry, carry on," Suzan said.

"The two rats didn't touch each other and didn't face each other; they only got close, so I assumed this virus mutated and is now airborne; only then did I look again at the microscope to find that the virus on the healthy rat…disappeared!"

Sarah seemed puzzled.

"Either I was confused, or the Camera had a glitch, so I isolated the healthy rat and got another one with the infected rat, and again, the same thing happened. In the beginning, I saw the virus at the throat, and then it disappeared again, and it happened with all the other rats except the last one, where the virus showed up and stayed."

He paused to ensure she could process all this information and then continued.

"Only then did I get the craziest idea and decided to try it!"

"What idea, David? What did you do?"

The Statue

The whole day, Joseph and Sarah talked about every piece and every statue at the Egyptian hall; they talked about every dynasty, every King and Pharaoh, and every Major incident that happened in ancient Egyptian history from King Narmer who unified Egypt and started the first dynasty circa 3150 B.C, then talking about the fourth dynasty around 2600 B.C when the Pyramids were built as they discussed different theories about who built them and how they were constructed, all the way until the Ptolemaic dynasty, and how it ended with Cleopatra's demise in 30 B.C.

John didn't want to interrupt the conversation, so he kept taking notes for his report and also added his remarks, but from time to time, he kept throwing some jokes whenever there was a chance, hoping that he would get Sarah's attention until it happened in front of one of the statues when their eyes caught each other. They had eye contact several times during the day, but this one was different; it was a second or less, but it was enough to make his heartbeat almost double as he fell into her wide black eyes. He could see that Sarah felt the same way; it was clear how her face blushed before she looked the other way, moving her hair behind her ears only to look more beautiful and increase John's Heart's beats even more.

John tried to break the silence. "It is almost 4:00 PM; time flies when one is in good company."

Then he smiled and looked at Joseph, "What do you think, Joseph? Did you have a good time?"

But Joseph was wholly lost looking at that statue in front of him; he was focusing on the statue's face and all the drawings crafted on what looked like a papyrus in the statue's right hand.

It wasn't like any other statue; one couldn't tell what he looked like exactly, with no eyes, nose, or ears. It was a pretty horrible sculpture; one couldn't define even the gender: tall and lean, the undefined face was looking up, one hand pointing down, the other holding some papers.

"Sarah, what is that?" Joseph asked.

"You mean, who is that? Most believe this is the statue of Akhenaten's personal servant."

She continued, "This statue belongs to the 18th dynasty when King Akhenaten ruled Egypt; there is nothing in history about this servant; we don't even know their name. All we know is this statue was found in Akhenaten's tomb next to the pharaoh's mummy, but no one knows what was special and why they kept it in the Pharaoh's holy tomb. We don't even know if this statue was one of the pharaoh's servants, but everything about Akhenaten was different from any other king in Egyptian history."

Joseph was still looking at the statue. "But his face looks weird; you can't tell how he looked. Was it found damaged like that? And why is he holding this papyrus?"

"It doesn't look like it was damaged; it looks like it was crafted like that, and maybe he was the Pharaoh's writer; he holds what looks like papyrus," John responded.

Sarah nodded her head while she looked at the statue. "You're right, John, about how the statue looks; it was not damaged, it was sculptured like that, and this is another puzzle from that era, but he was not the pharaoh's writer; otherwise, the statue would be sitting. Also, Nefertiti wrote all of Akhenaten's letters; he trusted none but her."

John looked at Sarah. "I would do the same if I was him."

"Also, this papyrus is just one repeated hieroglyphic alphabet over and over, and that's another puzzle!" Sarah replied as she was smiling.

Joseph looked at Sarah. "I noticed that on the papyrus, but that looks weird; maybe one day I will discover this statue's secret."

Sarah looked straight into his eyes and replied in a serious voice, "I am sure you will."

Then she smiled and continued, "Thank you. I had a great day."

"Me too," said John.

It's time for the VIP tour!" said Sarah.

Joseph's eyes widened and excited while John squinted and looked at Sarah. "VIP tour! I thought we visited every part of the Egyptian hall."

Sarah looked at John and smiled in a way that made John ready to follow her to the end of the world. "Not every part; there is still one part that is only for VIP visitors and needs an approval pass besides a background check before you can see it, but I can make an exception."

"Only if that will not cause you any trouble."

"Don't worry, all I need is to inform my professor, Dr. Jacob. Wait for me here; I will call him."

John looked at Sarah as she walked a few steps away while Joseph looked back at the statue and then pressed John's hand!

"What is wrong, Joseph? Are you OK?"

Joseph whispered, "Uncle John, take a picture of this statue and focus on the papyrus part."

John smiled. He sounded like an actor in an adventure movie, "OK, my friend, you know taking photos is not allowed here, but I will do my best; cover me."

"Mission accomplished," John said in a victorious tone.

Joseph chuckled. "Good job, Uncle John!"

Smiling, Sarah walked to them and said, "OK, Mission accomplished."

John paused as Sarah used the exact words, then asked in a bemused voice, "Mission!!… What Mission?"

Sarah looked at him, laughing. "Getting Dr. Jacob's permission to give you the special VIP tour."

John laughed nervously. "Oh, Great." John turned to Sarah and asked, "What is that thing you want us to visit?"

Sarah leaned forward, "Akhenaten's Coffin."

John and Joseph almost screamed in chorus, "What is it here?"

Sarah looked at Joseph, admiring his knowledge and curiosity. "The Tomb is made of pure gold, and we can't risk showing it in the main hall; that is why it's in a special room! Are you ready for this unique experience?"

Joseph looked at John, "This is the best day of my life!"

John looked at Sarah and said, "Mine too, Joseph."

Sarah blushed and acted like she was fixing her hair before she walked to a small room in a dark corner at the end of the hall. "OK, let's go; we don't want to keep the pharaoh waiting for us!"

They felt goosebumps but followed her to meet—The Pharaoh.

Pandemic

Suzan felt anxious.

"What? You did what?"

"Are you insane? Did you forget everything we learned about safety protocols? Why did you do that?"

"Suzan, if my theory is right, no one is safe!" David said in a calm voice.

Suzan took a deep breath. "Okay, David, so you injected your throat with a nanochip Camera; what next?"

"What is next depends on both of us."

Suzan forgot all her concerns as her scientific instinct jumped onto the surface. "I am listening."

David smiled as he noticed the change in her altered tone. "I scratched the idea that this virus is airborne; otherwise, we would see an enormous rising number of cases, so I took a blood sample from the infected rat and confirmed it's testing positive."

"OK, so how do you explain the virus was showing in the healthy rats without physical contact and just by having both in close proximity? I mean, air droplets would be an option, right?"

"There were no air droplets. I was monitoring the contained cage with another camera, and it's confirmed; nothing was in the air, which wiped off both ideas of air droplets and airborne."

Suzan, still confused, "Then how did the virus transfer…?"

She paused, then continued, "Also, how did the virus disappear again in all the rats except the last one?" She looked at David as if she understood something. "Wait…Why did you take the rat's blood sample? What will you do?"

"Suzan, I think this Virus has already invaded everyone's body. It's only waiting for the right time to show up!"

"What do you mean by invaded everyone's body? And how is it waiting for the right time to show up? You are baffling me."

David replied calmly, "This Virus is somehow… communicating."

Suzan looked at David as if she was watching someone who had lost his mind.

David continued, "OK, I want you to put the code of the nano camera and start monitoring my throat for any abnormal activities. Also, send the test results on time to the lab computer to confirm my results are positive."

Suzan was still looking at him and repeated her question, "Why did you take the blood sample?"

"Because I will expose myself to this blood sample."

Suzan was about to scream, but David spoke before she could. "But I need you to know something before we start this experiment."

Without saying another word, he took off his mask and Suzan's mask, too. Then, he put his hands around her neck and kissed her.

Suzan was flabbergasted by David's move, but she didn't stop him. For a moment, she forgot everything about the virus and the experiment and just lived this second, feeling David's hand moving on her neck and pressing it gently.

David stepped back and said, "I'm sorry, Suzan, I…"

Suzan smiled and replied in a hurry, "Don't be. But you are crazy; I can't let you risk your life."

"We must figure out what this thing is, Suzan; otherwise, we will never be able to stop it."

Without saying another word, David walked to the isolated room in the lab without his face mask, and Suzan put her mask back on and took her seat in front of the monitor.

David took the blood sample from the isolated container and held it.

"Anything on the Monitor, Suzan?"

"I don't see any activity on the throat. It looks like your theory is proved wrong."

"Just keep looking closely."

For about five minutes, there was nothing on the monitor.

"Try to remove the mask; you may see things more clearly."

Suzan was unconvinced but decided to go with David's theory to see the result.

She took off her mask, but at the exact moment, and without her noticing, David opened the door of the isolated room.

Suzan was focused entirely on the monitor, and in a confident voice, she said, "You saw the activity on the camera right away when the rats got closer to each other, and you have been holding this sample for more than five minutes, and there is no…"

She stopped talking and screamed, "OH MY GOD…What was that?"

On the monitor, a massive number of viruses on the throat showed up out of nowhere for just one second and then disappeared again like they were never there.

David sealed the sample again and left the isolated room. He put his mask on first before moving towards Suzan, who was shaking with fear. She was terrified!

"David, I never saw anything like this; this is impossible; it showed up and disappeared and…"

"And what, Suzan?"

"When I saw this thing on the monitor, my whole body shook, and I felt pain in my throat; I was scared. Are you OK? Do you feel any pain?"

David put his hands on her shoulders. "I am alright, Suzan, but what you saw on the monitor was not my throat… It was …yours."

Suzan was perplexed. "Wait…What…How…You!"

She stood up and slapped David on his face. "That is why you kissed me! So, you can inject the camera into my throat! How dare you?"

She started crying.

David leaned on his knees in front of her.

"Suzan, this kiss was the best thing that happened in my life. There were many ways to inject this camera in your throat, but I was not sure what would happen to me after this experiment, and I wanted to kiss you even if this was the last thing I would do."

Suzan looked at him with teary eyes, and he could feel her expression even behind the mask. "Wait, this means the virus infected me, but how did it appear and disappear like that, and why didn't you monitor your throat? Did you even inject yourself?"

"One day at a time, Suzan. Let's find answers to all these questions one by one."

The Pharaoh

"Run Joseph…. RUN."

John shouted aloud while running towards his car in the parking lot, and Joseph was running next to him!

Wait….

John stopped typing, his face looking confused, before he muttered to himself, "I think I escaped an hour before we ran to the car."

Let us go back on time a little bit, not too much, just one hour…

John and Joseph followed Sarah through the door at the corner of the Egyptian Hall; the door led them to a small room. The lights were dim, and there was nothing except some ancient drawings on the walls, but in the middle of this room, there it was!

The Golden Coffin of King Akhenaten.

For a moment, they both froze, looking at this magnificent coffin that the museum had kept safe in this room to protect it from attempts of robbery or vandalism!

Joseph was astounded and reluctant to move closer to the coffin. "Is this real gold?" Joseph asked as he looked at the Coffin, his eyes wide open.

Sarah proudly said, "Yes, Joseph, I saw this coffin a hundred times, and I am still amazed how they made it that perfect."

John looked at the coffin while writing notes, then at Sarah and asked, "Do you think I can take a picture of this Coffin? It'll be an amazing picture on the first page of our newspaper."

Sarah winked at him and said, "Pictures are not allowed, but I guess if you took one, I couldn't stop you."

John smiled and took out his phone. He snapped a couple of captures, but in the second photo, he zoomed in on a specific part of the casket that didn't look right to him.

"Show me," Sarah said.

"It doesn't look that good; I deleted it. Let me take another one."

He snapped a few more of the coffin and the room, then showed her the phone.

"What do you think?"

Sarah pointed at one of the pictures, "This looks great. I can't wait to see it in the newspaper."

The coffin was made of pure gold, with drawings all over it, inside and outside. These drawings told the King's stories, victories, battles, marriage, and new religion. Everything was in harmony except that part at one corner of the coffin; it looked like some random hieroglyphic symbols but started with a sign that kept repeating every few symbols without a clear pattern.

Joseph looked at Sarah and was about to ask her about this part of the coffin, but then he noticed his uncle's eyes. Something in his eyes told him to stop. Joseph decided not to talk!

Sarah noticed the concern in Joseph's eyes, "Hey Joseph, what do you think about our pharaoh?"

"Majestic."

He tried to hide his concerns, but Sarah insisted, "Do you have any questions?"

John jumped between the conversation, trying to save his nephew from Sarah's questions. "I do have a question; where is the Mummy?"

"The Mummy will arrive in a few days; many arrangements must be completed."

She continued, "This Mummy was a huge discovery in 1907, thanks to Edward Ayrton and his crew for this great discovery, don't you agree, Joseph?"

Joseph looked pale, and Sarah was concerned. "Joseph, you look tired. Are you OK?"

Nervous, Joseph looked toward John and said, "Uncle John, I don't feel well. Can we leave?"

John replied quickly, "Yes, I think we should go, you look tired, Joseph; it was a long day."

"Sarah, thank you for this amazing day. I will call you tomorrow to discuss the technical details for the article."

"Sure, I'll wait for your call."

She looked at Joseph. "You need to get some rest, my friend. I am sure we will meet again."

Joseph nodded with a nervous smile on his face.

"I guess you will have a long night writing your article?"

"Yes, I need to start it tonight, but I will finish it when we meet again so that I can use your help on some historical information."

Sarah smiled while the security guard opened the door. As they reached the door, John took another look at the room, but he was not looking at the coffin this time; he was looking at that part of the room where Joseph was staring.

"Are you feeling better now?" John asked as they left the room.

"Yes, I think the small room nauseated me; fresh air will help."

"Thank you, Sarah, you made this day very special for both of us." He shook her hand.

"Same here, John. I enjoyed being with you and Joseph today."

She looked at Joseph. "I can't wait to see you next time, buddy."

Joseph said nothing, went straight to Sarah, and hugged her. Sarah hugged him back, and from afar, you could see her eyes sparkle with tears. They stayed for a few seconds before Joseph looked at her and said, "Thank you."

She smiled, turned, and walked without looking back.

Joseph and John looked at her briefly before looking at each other.

Joseph felt confused, like he had just awakened from a dream, and then started talking, "Did you notice the coffin?"

"Yes, that was a smart move when you didn't ask her about it."

"Uncle John, there was someone else in this room."

"I think we have a lot to talk about. Tonight, partner."

"Do you know what will get your energy back?"

"What, Uncle John?"

"Racing to the car, if you win, you can have Pizza for dinner."

Run Joseph… RUN…

The Sign

"Mom… we're back."

John and Joseph walked through the front door while John was checking a message on his phone. Suzan was sitting by the dining table in the kitchen with a mug of coffee.

Joseph ran to his mother to hug her. Suzan stepped back, pushing him away, "Joseph, I feel sick. I don't want you to catch anything."

"It's OK, mom. I hope you feel better soon."

"Mom, you wouldn't believe our exciting visit to the museum!"

"I can't wait to hear the details, but first go and shower, then we can talk at dinner."

John stopped checking his phone and looked at Joseph, "Don't take too long, I'm hungry; I ordered Pizza."

Joseph chuckled and ran upstairs to shower while John looked at his sister and asked her worriedly, "Is this a cup of coffee? Suzan, are you OK?"

Suzan dropped on the chair, looking at her brother. "I'm OK, John, you tell me. Is everything OK? You keep checking your phone."

"Yes, all's good. Terry was texting me, asking about my day. He never checks on me when I am working on a report," John replied. "We had a good time, me and Joseph; he was happy, and he sounded excited. This is not how Terry usually responds, but forget about him now and tell me what's wrong. You look exhausted!"

"Sit down, John; I need to tell you about my day before Joseph comes back."

She told John about David, his experiment, and the nano-chip camera when John interrupted her, "So, he kissed you?!"

Suzan raised her eyebrow, looking at him. "Really…from all I told you, that grabbed your attention?!"

Without waiting for his response, she continued to tell him about the experiment.

This time, John looked worried. "Are you telling me you are infected by this virus?"

Suzan answered in a dispersed voice, "I don't know. I am baffled as I am now involved in this mess with David, and I don't know what to do. But I tested myself before leaving the lab; this is routine; to test in the morning and before we leave, and it showed negative, but at this moment, I am not sure what we're testing and if this test result means anything."

"We didn't follow any safety protocols. Besides, we overused the nanochip cameras. Do you know how much each one cost? We used eight cameras on this experiment, talking about millions of dollars without authorization!"

John looked at her, confused; he asked, "If I didn't miss anything, then you only used seven cameras, right? Five on the rats, then David and you, so where is the eighth camera?"

"Here, I brought it with me!"

"Why?"

"Because I want to inject it in Joseph's throat to check him.!"

"But Joseph hasn't shown any symptoms."

"And I didn't show any symptoms, nor did David, but we both still carry this virus, even knowing we both tested negative. I am sure you, too, are a carrier. It's like this virus is hiding and waiting."

"Waiting for what?"

"I don't know… I'm sure David will have some answers tonight."

She said that while holding her phone and dialing David's number.

"He's not answering."

John tried to calm her. "He probably hasn't checked the files yet, or maybe he checked it and didn't find anything to worry about."

Before he said more, they heard Joseph screaming aloud. They ran upstairs to find Joseph standing in the middle of the bathroom, with his eyes wide open and his towel around his waist.

"Joseph, what's happened? Are you OK?" Suzan panicked.

Without saying a word or looking at her, Joseph pointed toward the bathroom mirror, where John looked precisely.

On the mirror was the same drawing of the symbol they saw on the Coffin.

Suzan looked to where Joseph was pointing, "What is that? And why do you look scared like that?"

John looked to Joseph straight into the eyes. "What happened here?"

Joseph said in a scared voice, "He was here, Uncle John; I was in the shower, and he just showed up in front of the mirror, and without even looking at me, he drew this sign and disappeared into thin air."

"Who was here? And what is so scary about this sign? What happened today at the museum?" Suzan felt impatient.

John patted her back before helping her to stand up, and then, holding Joseph's hand, he said, "I will explain everything to you, Suzan, but let's have dinner first. It wasn't just you who had an extraordinary day, and we, too, had some fun at the museum!"

He looked at Joseph and smiled. "Looks like you are about to discover something; apparently, it runs in this family."

Over dinner, Suzan was looking at Joseph. "How are you feeling now?"

Joseph was still worried but didn't want to display his fears to his mom and uncle.

"I am okay, Mom!"

"Joseph, I want you to listen to me. I can tell you that everything is OK, and we can ignore what happened, hoping you will forget about it within a day or two. I can also tell you what you saw was just an illusion because of what we saw at the museum today, which could be the case, but no, Joseph, I will not say that. You are the one who discovered this sign, and you are the one who saw the hidden message in the coffin. We are dealing with something supernatural, but whatever we face, it doesn't want to hurt you. I think this supernatural power needs your help. I think they are trying to guide you to something. Now, will we work on this together, or else we'll be terrified? Remember, you can run, but you can't hide. So, let's face it together. Okay?"

John was talking to himself more than talking to Joseph. Deep inside, He felt scared; he wished to ignore all that and act as if it had never happened. But another part inside him was pushing him forward, a part inside him that kept saying, "That's it, this is the story you've been waiting for, this is the moment, this is your chance to start the adventure that you always wished for."

What he said worked perfectly for him and Joseph. He was less scared and more excited to figure out the truth; Joseph's feeling was the same.

Joseph looked eager, "This is a quiz, and I will solve it." He paused briefly before continuing, "We will solve it!"

Suzan smiled at John and said, "You'll make a great Dad."

Then she looked at Joseph and said, "Now, tell me about the Museum."

Joseph looked at her and then looked back at John.

"The thing I saw in the bathroom was also at the coffin chamber; it was hiding in the dark corner, but…" He paused briefly before saying, "But it looked like he wanted me to see him!"

John patted his back. "I know Joseph…I know; I saw him, too."

Suzan looked confused. "I am sure these are illusions; I really need to know what happened at the museum?"

He waited until Joseph went upstairs, and then he looked at Suzan. "It was not an illusion." He showed her the photos on his phone, and in one of those photos, in the dark corner, was that! It was there… the statue."

Suzan looked at him in awe. "This statue could be just there; what is wrong with that?"

John brought his phone closer to her eyes and showed her the photos of the same corner; the statue was still there, except in different positions; in the other images, it had vanished.

Suzan gasped as she looked at her phone when it buzzed with a video message before looking at John. "John, this is a video message from David. Why didn't he call?"

She waited for an answer to her question before opening the message.

What appeared on the video message was frightening…

Invasion

Los Angeles - California

Wednesday March 5th, 2025

Time 5:00 PM

David drove back home with a million thoughts and ideas in his mind.

As he reached home, without wasting time, he went straight to his lab, where the electronic microscope was still connected to his computer.

He switched it on and went to the file with the serial no of the nano camera in his throat.

"Moment of truth." He muttered.

David clicked on the file. In the beginning, as he expected, there was nothing except the typical image of the throat, then suddenly the screen was filled with what looked like the virus; it showed out of nowhere all over the screen and stayed there for a second before it disappeared.

Even though David was expecting what he saw, it was still scary, as, this time, he was looking at something inside his body.

His phone rang.

It was Suzan.

He glanced at the phone with a smile full of love.

"Suzan, I'll have to call you with some exciting news after I am done. Okay?" He almost mumbled.

With that said, he split the image on the monitor into two sections; one showed the camera in his throat, and the other half showed the camera in Suzan's throat. He set the time to move frame by frame and programmed the computer to capture any differences between the two images.

He monitored closely for twenty minutes, and then a smile of victory embraced his face… Both cameras suddenly showed the virus on the same frame.

He looked closely at the monitor of both cameras, only to see the virus on Suzan's camera disappear, but on his camera, it stayed for a second longer before disappearing.

"This virus is invading everybody; we are all infected; there was no time for the virus to travel all this distance between Suzan and me. It communicated as soon as I opened the door, and she removed the mask, but how come the body didn't react to it? There were no symptoms, and why did it appear and then disappear in others? And how did the virus know we are not wearing a mask or are in an isolated room, unless…" He paused for a second, then continued, "unless this virus can see what we are seeing!"

He tried to align his thoughts.

"OK, David, you call it an invasion, as this virus was able to infect everybody, but you are going too far now; how can the virus see what we see and know we are wearing a mask or not?"

He switched the computer to monitor the camera in his throat while the other half of the screen still showed Suzan's camera record. Then, he moved the frames right before the frame where the virus showed up. He put on his mask, moved the frames forward to show the virus on Suzan's screen, and checked his camera as there were no activities. Then, he looked closely at Suzan's screen and took off his mask, and only then did his camera start showing a massive number of the virus, but this time, the virus didn't disappear!

David kept looking, and then he saw what scared him to death. The virus starts taking a form, and all the viruses blend into a giant shape.

David was sweating and could hardly speak aloud. "This thing can't be a virus. It can see us, and it can hear us." …this is…."

His throat started swelling, and he felt his body temperature rising rapidly.

He went to his phone and started recording a video.

His voice, barely audible.

"Suzan… it's coming after you, this isn't…"

Moments later, his voice was completely gone, and his body started turning red as blood was coming out from his nose and his mouth. He fell on the floor, still holding the phone. He wiped the blood and started drawing on the floor a shape that the virus blended to form…. He drew a sign, the same sign from the museum

Night Visit

"How is she doing now?" Joseph asked in a concerned voice.

John smiled and put his hand on Joseph's head, "She'll be fine; she's had a long day, like us."

"Uncle John, I am scared; I can't stop thinking about what I saw in the bathroom. May I sleep in your room tonight?"

"Joseph, I was about to ask you the same thing: if I can sleep in yours tonight, but what about tomorrow or the day after or when I go back to New York? What you saw could be just an illusion, but even if it was real, it doesn't want to hurt us; it wants us to focus on…"

Joseph finished his uncle's sentence. "On the sign…Right?"

"Yes, there is something about this sign and the whole inscription that we saw at the museum; there is a link between this sign and the virus."

"The virus…How?"

John didn't want to tell him about what they saw on the video, so he looked at him and just said, "It's just a hunch…but we'll understand more when we translate these inscriptions."

"You're right; I will focus on this task. I may even surprise you."

"I'm sure you will, but you need to rest now, and we'll work on it tomorrow."

"Okay. Goodnight, Uncle John."

"Nighty night, Joseph."

John sat on the chair next to the couch where Suzan was lying down.

"The virus, the sign, the museum, Terry, Sarah…there is a link between all of this."

He looked in front of him as if he was talking to someone. "Why did you send me here, Terry…Why?"

"John, we need to go to David's house."

"Suzan, are you awake? You should rest. We will talk tomorrow."

"There is no time; we have to go; we have to get the electronic microscope and the computer."

Suzan was muttering between pauses. Clearly, she was scared.

"Suzan, you want us to break into his house knowing he could be dead because of a virus that you might be infected by as well...do you hear yourself?"

"John, the first thing they will do after discovering the body will be to check the microscope, which will trace the camera I have in my throat."

"Is there a way to remove this camera?"

"Yes, but I need to continue what David started; I am not letting his Death be in vain."

She continued, "David was very close to solving this mystery. I will not wait until both of us are accused of embezzlement, and I will not run away and ruin all his efforts. I must continue his work and clear his name; otherwise, I will end up in jail."

She couldn't stop her tears. "Do you think he's dead?"

"I hope not, Suzan, I hope not." John pulled himself together to calm his sister.

"OK, Suzan, I'll go. I assume you have his address?"

"Yes, I do, but before you go, I need to see the drawings from the museum. Please send them to me; we must find the link between this sign and the virus. I will go upstairs to check on Joseph and speak with him about his day at the museum."

"I printed it out on the 3D printer. Don't exhaust yourself and take it easy; remember David's last words: *it is coming for you!* I don't know what that means, but be careful, and don't forget to keep your mask around Joseph; I am not sure if that makes a difference now."

"It always makes a difference...Always." Suzan mumbled

Then she continued, "How are you going to break into his house?"

"Your brother has some skills," John winked.

It took him around an hour before he parked near David's house. He walked around the place, looking for an open window, but they were all shut. He moved to the front door, and in a desperate move, he tried to open it.

John was surprised when he found the door was not locked, and the next second, he found himself inside the house.

He put on his gloves and tried to find his way to the lab, and it didn't take him long to find the microscope and the computer that Suzan had described. He also took all of David's notes; everything was there, everything except one thing. It was missing...David's body.

The Affair

"What do you mean his body was not there? We both saw what happened in the video message." Suzan was in panic mode.

"Yes, Suzan, we both saw the video, but I am telling you what happened: the floor was clean, with no blood stains or any drawings, and his body was not there; it was nowhere in the house."

"Then he may be alive; he must've left the house. He will call me back to tell me where he is, or I'll call him." She rushed for her phone.

John looked at his sister sadly. He didn't want to ruin her hopes, but it didn't take long before she dropped on the couch and cried as David's phone went straight to the voicemail.

"His phone is switched off. Why did he turn his phone off, dammit?"

John sat next to her and hugged her; she put her head on his chest. John kept holding her and tried to calm her down.

"Suzan, I don't know if David is still alive or not, but we both saw him on that video, and we both know that no one can survive what we saw; the house door was open, the floor was clean, and all the equipment and notes were there, this all leads to one conclusion."

"Someone took David's body; someone is trying to frame David with something…" Suzan replied in a perplexed tone.

"And that someone knows about us and left us all the equipment and notes! Whoever did that knew we would go to David's house." John continued as he nodded his head.

Suzan looked at him helplessly.

"Even If David was still alive, he couldn't escape what could hurt him. You can escape the enemy from outside, but not the enemy inside. The only way to defeat the enemy within you is to clear your mind and step back to see the big picture. Only then can you see how this enemy thinks and reacts, and only then would you know how to win. I think that is what David did; he discovered something, and whatever he discovered was the reason for his death or disappearance," John continued.

"You're right; I need to let my emotions aside and continue with David's research," Suzan replied as she started to pull herself together.

She went straight to another room that she designed as her lab and took David's computer, notes, and the microscope with her before she looked back to John, saying, "I don't know what we're looking for, but we're running out of time, they will notice David's absence soon, and that will lead to the missing microscope. I'll have to return it as soon as possible. I'll work on the notes, and you'll need to work on breaking the code of the pharaoh's inscriptions. I heard about what happened from Joseph before he went to sleep. We need to work on two directions simultaneously, and I am sure those two directions will interconnect."

She kept walking to the lab and then turned and looked at her brother lovingly.

"John, I am glad you are here with us; I don't know how I would survive all of this without you. I am glad Terry sent you here, even if it was for the wrong reasons..."

"What do you mean by wrong reasons? Suzan, is there something you are hiding? This is not the time for riddles; we are dealing with many mysteries, so please don't add another one to the list."

"Your visit to the museum is for a reason, and I am sure now it has something to do with the Virus, but..."

"But what?"

Suzan paused before she spoke fast as if she wanted to get rid of something she was holding in her chest.

"Terry and Laura are having an affair."

"What!!! An Affair? Terry ...Laura...This is impossible. Is that why you got divorced? Is that the reason you avoided talking to her all this time?"

"Yes, that is why I got divorced, and that is why I stopped talking to her or about her with anyone, and yes, they're having an affair, and that is why he sent you here, so he can have more time with her…at least that is what I thought."

John looked super confused. "More time with her? Why did he need to send me all the way here to have more time with her?"

Suzan looked at him surprisingly, "Because Laura is your girlfriend!"

John looked at her with a perplexed face, "Laura is my neighbor. She was never my girlfriend, and you know that.!"

"Your neighbor! What are you talking about? I avoided discussing what happened between Terry and Laura for years because I worried about you. I warned them not to mention anything to you and told Laura to stay away from you. What do you mean she was never your girlfriend? You guys were together for years, but you broke up at the end of 2020, right after the pandemic, after she recovered from…"

"Suzan, I don't know what you're talking about; listen, we're all tired, and we had a long, insane day, and I feel tomorrow will bring more action. It would be best to get your thoughts together to solve this virus mystery case. Let's all sleep, and in the morning, we'll call Terry and Laura to clear things up. Okay?" John interrupted her in a firm tone.

Suzan nodded, agreeing, and walked upstairs, but her face was perplexed before she turned back to him, saying, "John, we will talk in the morning, but there is something else I want to tell you."

John looked at her with a smile. "What is it, sister?"

"This sign from the Museum…I've seen it before."

"I am sure you saw it before; we all saw it before; it is a famous sign…"

She interrupted him, "No, John, this sign looks a bit different, and I saw it before."

"Where... When?" John asked, confused.

"We'll talk tomorrow… It's a long, confusing story." With that, she went upstairs, leaving John with a million questions that will not get him any sleep."

Laura

Brooklyn – New York

Wednesday, March 5th, 2025

Time 7:00 PM

"Would you like something else to drink?" the waiter asked.

Laura smiled. "No, thank you. I'm good."

She was going to ask the waiter about something but then changed her mind and said, "Never mind, Thanks."

She picked up her purse and left the coffee shop. She walked outside and then turned to look at herself on the big glass window of the coffee shop to fix her dress. At that moment, she saw his reflection in the window as he crossed the street and moved towards her with quick steps.

"You're late; where else should we meet so you won't be late?" Her voice was cold.

"I'm sorry, I had to take care of a few things and thought I'd be back on time. Give me two minutes," Terry replied while trying to catch his breath.

He walked into the coffee shop and talked to the waiter before he went back outside, holding a cup of water.

"OK, you said we need to talk; what's going on?"

"Here!! Are we going to talk here?

"Let's walk to my place, it's nearby."

She answered with a sarcastic smile, "I know." The smile faded away quickly as she felt something wrong.

They both walked without saying a word until they reached Terry's apartment. Terry opened the door and invited Laura in with a hand gesture and a smile; then, he closed the door and walked to an oversized couch next to the door. He sat down and took a big sip of his water cup before looking at Laura.

"Now we can talk; what is going on?"

Laura sat on her knees in front of him, and without saying a word, she put her hands around his face and leaned forward to kiss him.

Terry gently moved her hands and pushed his face away from her.

"Laura, I think we need to put an end to this. This relationship is awkward; it was a mistake that already cost me my wife and my kid."

Laura stood up and walked around Terry's small apartment, her steps heavy and slow. She looked at the ceiling before stopping and looked straight into Terry's eyes.

"Terry, how long have we been together?"

Terry looked confused, "I think five years, as far as I can remember, why?"

"Yes, as far as you can remember, and I remember, and also Suzan remembers it's been five years." Laura came closer; her tone was strange.

"And?" Terry asked.

"How did it start, when was the first time, where was it, how did Suzan know about it, how come John didn't find out?" How come...."

She stopped and fell on the couch, and started sobbing.

Terry sat next to her and surrounded her with his arms. She shook while talking, "How come I don't feel your kiss, but my memories say something else?"

Terry hugged her tight, trying to be calm and hide his worries, "I wish I had an answer to all these questions, but I am sure we'll figure it out soon, especially after…"

Laura looked at him, interrupting, "After the dream, right?"

Terry nodded his head while moving his arms away from her. and looking at nowhere. "Yes, something scary is happening; you and I had the same dream on the same night. It was like a nightmare when I dreamed about this guy with a weird, undefined face like you can't tell what they look like; you can't even tell if it's a human or an alien." He paused and then said in a deep voice, "I was frightened when this creature said to me, *'The answers to all your questions are with the pharaoh; send John to the museum and send him to Suzan!'*."

"I woke up thinking about this weird dream, and only in the morning did I find you calling me and telling me you had the same dream. I had to send John to California. I don't know how that will answer all these questions, but I feel we did the right thing."

"What if they want to hurt John?" Laura sounded frightened.

"They? Who are they? And why would they want to hurt him?"

Laura looked at him as if she'd just remembered something. "Hey, did you call John today?"

"Usually, I don't call him when he is working on a report; I don't want to do anything suspicious. I am guessing he stopped by Suzan and talked to her about his visit to the Museum. I am sure Joseph will be so excited about his uncle's visit, especially if he took him there, and…" Terry stopped talking with a terrifying look in his eyes, while Laura mumbled, "Oh my God…Joseph!"

Terry picked up the phone and texted John. But then her face looked relieved as John replied to the text message.

"They are okay and already home; John said the report he is making about the museum will be a surprise."

Laura had a slight smile on her face. But the smile vanished, and she seemed consumed by an idea.

Terry sat next to her. "What's on your mind?"

"A crazy idea, but it's the only explanation that could make all this madness make sense."

Jacob

Los Angeles - California

Wednesday March 5th, 2025

Time 6:00 PM

Sarah took the elevator to the third floor in the small building next to the exhibit. Then she walked to an office with a sign that read, "Dr. Ed Jacob." She took a deep breath before knocking and heard a voice from inside.

"Come in, Sarah."

Sarah entered, quite surprised. "How did you know I am at the door, Dr. Jacob?"

He smiled back at her. "Sarah…You are the only polite person in this building who still knocks and waits for an answer….no one else does that."

"Also, I can see you on this camera." Dr. Jacob pointed toward the camera.

Sarah paused for a second as she had this weird feeling that this conversation had happened before. She mumbled, "Dejavu," then shrugged her shoulder and smiled while looking at the screen on the desk.

In his early sixties, Dr. Jacob was tall and lean and had sharp eyes like an eagle. His eyes matched his long-hooked nose and bald head perfectly, except for some white hair on the sideburns.

He is like a Godfather to Sarah since he hired and trained her long ago when Sarah joined the team.

"So, Sarah…How is the day going…all good?"

"Yes…everything went as planned—he managed to take photos of the inscription."

Jacob smiled. "I know, Sarah, I saw it on this screen; I am asking about you. You look perplexed."

"I think we are making a mistake."

"What mistake?"

"We should not interfere; we need to let things be, and we don't know if they will make the right choice…"

Jacob interrupted her with a firm look. "We know, Sarah, we are here because we know, and we are not interfering; we are just monitoring."

"When we are monitoring, we are interfering, and it is not an easy decision as every time we move on, something different happens, and the whole scenario changes…. They have a right to choose."

"Choose what, Sarah. This ship sailed a long time ago. You know how many times we talked about this decision, and you also know how many times we delayed it, and you know why we have to take this decision. If they fail this last quiz, it's the end; you knew that since day one…. And you know that you are the reason behind everything, all since day one…remember?!"

"Yes, I remember."

A phone call interrupted the conversation. Dr. Jacob answered the phone.

Even with his reputation of emotional constancy, Sarah could notice the concerned look in his eyes!

Jacob finished the call, saying, "OK, take all precautions and clean it up."

"What happened?"

"Looks like you were right, Sarah; something different happens every time we move on."

He got his calm tone back before he looked at her, emphasizing, "We have casualties…David is dead."

"What…David?!! But he was supposed to…"

"Sarah…. I know what he was supposed to do, but as you'd said, this is a dynamic game, and things keep changing; we now need a replacement. However, it is a minor change, and we should get things back on track. You will need to contact John first thing tomorrow as planned."

"Minor change!! How did he die? And who was on the phone? It was him…Right? It was his call to kill David; this is breaking all codes! We are supposed to supervise; we can't interact. That was rule one. Why are you allowing this? What happened to…"

"We are not interfering; we are monitoring!" Jacob interrupted her. "Sarah…we are all in this together. He is part of this team and had to make this call. If you are wondering, it wasn't my decision, but I would do the same if it were my call. You need to look at the big picture; David's research went a different route, and we had to stop it."

Sarah nodded desperately before she asked, "Who is the replacement?"

"Suzan."

"Suzan, but Suzan was supposed to…"

"Sarah, I know what was supposed to have happened, and I told you we have minor changes. You must focus on your role and let everyone else do their job."

Sarah looked down and sighed. She turned to leave and then turned back to Dr. Jacob, "I think it's time for some recalculation." With that, she went and closed the door behind her. She was planning to meet John tomorrow, but for a different reason than Jacob wanted.

Dr. Jacob muttered, "OK, it's time for some minor changes, perhaps recalculation, as they say!"

Then he muttered, "Recalculation…maybe."

At the exact moment, his phone rang. He picked up and listened to the person on the other side before replying angrily, "Clean this mess!"

He hung up, took a piece of paper, and started drawing a pyramid. He wrote some numbers before he tore the paper and threw it in the trashcan.

"Maybe not." He muttered.

Memories

"What??... Mandela Effect...What are you talking about?"

Laura looked at Terry before she stood up and sat on a chair in front of him, looking him straight in the eyes.

"I need you to listen and think how both of us and Suzan are sharing a memory about me and you, having an affair for years, but at the same time, we both don't feel anything when we kiss each other, and we don't remember the basic details about this relationship, like, how did it start, or where or when…"

Terry looked at her. "OK! keep talking."

Laura leaned back and started to feel like she was doing her job explaining to one of her patients about her case.

"Do you know Nelson Mandela?"

"Yes, he was a former South African activist and politician. Why?"

"OK, when did he die?"

"Wait… what… is this a history test or something?!"

"Just answer, please!"

"I remember he died in the 1980s; not sure about the exact year, but there was a huge amount of coverage in the news." Terry paused for a second and then continued…

"And our Former President Obama attended the memorial service." Terry paused as his face looked confused and perplexed.

"Exactly; our former president Obama attended the memorial service because Nelson Mandela was the former South African president and died in 2013. But you shouldn't feel bad about yourself because it is not just you who thought that Nelson Mandela died in the 1980s." there are vast groups of people from different backgrounds and different careers and education levels. All of them will give the same answer; all of them will think that Mandela died in the 1980s until another memory from 2013 hits them, and they will give the same facial reaction that you had on your face a few seconds ago."

Still confused, Terry said, "OK, would you please stop giving lectures and tell me how this story fits into our situation?"

"Don't you see it? The three of us could have The Mandela Effect, where we remember things differently than the truth!"

Terry looked very confused. Laura continued, "Like people remember the famous line from Star Wars differently or the spelling from Looney Toons, whereas it is actually Looney Tunes, or…"

Terry looked disappointed. "Or what?"

She continued, "Or it is a form of Confabulation!"

Terry looked like a mix of frustration and anger. "Confabulation!! And what is that now?"

"This is when you mix between imagination and reality and fill the gaps in your memory, or when someone keeps talking about a place and adds all the details and feelings to the point where you believe that it was you and not the other person that has been at this place before, did you feel that before?"

Terry seemed more relaxed, accepting the idea. "Yes, like *déjà vu,* when you feel you have seen this place before or you went through the same situation before."

"Exactly, and most of the time, it is because someone was talking about it, and you kept imagining it, and then your memory starts saving it as reality—that is, Confabulation."

"OK, I like this theory, but again, how does it fit into our situation? This "Mandela Effect" theory is happening to larger groups of people, and it doesn't change the course of events dramatically; it is like we miss a sentence in a movie or a letter, on a logo or a date of someone's death, but not the whole scenario about an affair! What is happening is not about other people, like celebrities; it is about us, and it is affecting only the three of us, and no one else has these memories about me and you having an affair." Terry paused to catch his breath.

"Then, that 'confabulation' explanation makes more sense in our situation. However, it is based on whether we were thinking about each other till we believed it was the reality, and that seems impossible because, as you said, we can't even feel a kiss. Besides, how can Suzan have the same memory? Or was there someone somehow talking about this affair to the three of us until our memory fit it in as reality, and again, this is impossible; who will talk about this and for how long, and how did …."

Terry stopped talking as his whole body started shivering with excitement—he knew he'd found out the truth.

Laura looked at him and said calmly, "The same person who visited me and you in dreams, but that means…"

Terry continued, "That means we need to talk to Suzan."

He turned to pick up his phone, but both of them froze, as next to the table was this dark shape who slowly walked to the spot.

Terry looked at the shape before shouting nervously, "You, how did you get in here?!"

Before he or Laura could say anything more, their bodies started shaking, and they fell on the floor, and blood oozed out from their mouths and noses.

The shape took a phone out of his pocket and dialed a number, "The equation is back and under control!"

He listened to the person on the other side and hung up.

Then, he started cleaning the mess.

Adam

Los Angeles - California

Thursday March 6th, 2025

Time 8:00 AM

Suzan went downstairs holding a big envelope to find John at the dining table covered with sticky notes. He looked consumed looking at them as he kept moving them side to side.

Suzan smiled at him before walking to the kitchen. "You are up early. Do you want some breakfast?"

Without looking at her and still moving the notes from side to side, John said, "I didn't sleep at all; I couldn't, especially after what you'd said last night; how is Joseph?"

"He was still awake in his bed when I checked on him. After talking to him, he went into deep sleep."

"Good, he has been through much yesterday. He is a smart, strong kid; you're lucky to have him." He paused for a second before continuing, "Are you okay to talk now?"

"Not for long, as I need to go to the lab. I have to work on David's notes."

"OK, I called Terry, and he didn't answer. I think he, Laura, and you owe me an explanation. I need to know how everyone except me thinks Laura is my girlfriend!"

Suzan looked at him with a smile on her face. "She was, John. Laura was your girlfriend!"

He was about to scream out of anger. Instead, he took a deep breath and said, "OK, I think this issue will clear itself later, but for now, we need to work on what happened yesterday between the museum and the virus inside your body and David's."

Suzan sounded despaired and sad. "Yes...David..." She held herself and continued, "As I told you yesterday, I saw this sign before."

"Yes, and you left me with many other questions; what did you mean you saw this sign before? This sign looks like an infinity symbol, or as they call it, lazy eight. It is a mathematical symbol; you have seen it before."

She grabbed a chair next to the dining table and sat down.

"Terry's great-grandfather Adam was born and raised in Egypt. We knew Joseph inherited his fondness of Egyptian history from Terry's great grandfather."

John looked at her with concern. "Yes, I know. You mentioned this to me a few years ago, but how is that related to the sign?"

She continued, "Adam was part of the crew working with Edward Ayrton in 1907. He was the one who discovered Akhenaten's mummy!"

John stood up, looking at his sister in shock. "Yes, how did I forget about Adam and that he was part of Edward's crew!"

"Same here. I totally forgot about it until yesterday."

Los Angeles - California

Monday, March 19, 2035

11:45 pm

John stopped typing and mumbled, "How come I forgot something like that? Did I actually forget about it? When I first met Sarah at the Museum, I remember not mentioning Joseph's grandfather's name; I knew he was part of Edward's crew, so why do I think I forgot about it!" He shook his head, took off his glasses, and wiped his face with his palms before fixing them on his face. Then, he took a deep breath and continued typing.

***

Los Angeles - California

Thursday March 6th, 2025

Time 8:15 AM

John looked at his sister and said, "OK, now, as we both remember, tell me where you saw this sign?"

She turned, grabbed the envelope, and put it in front of John. "Here, this will answer your questions."

"What is that?"

"This is Adam's diary. Terry inherited it and gave it to me a long time ago, and I was waiting to give it to Joseph at the right time. It is over a hundred years old, so be careful; each paper is wrapped in plastic to keep it in good shape."

John looked impressed while opening the envelope. "This could be the answer to this riddle."

Suzan mumbled, "Or it could be another riddle."

She continued in an embarrassed voice, "I never read it all, neither did Terry. I usually browsed without paying attention to detail and kept it as an antique. But yesterday, I remembered seeing the sign while browsing through the pages, but then again, I was swamped with the virus. So…"

"I feel stupid not to have read it a long time ago." She completed after the pause.

John looked at her empathetically, then opened the diary and started reading… "The Journey by Adam Sadek…"

He stopped and looked at her, "Don't be hard on yourself; at least you kept it safe. And that in itself means something. Alright?"

She smiled and nodded. He looked back at the diary and started reading.

The diary talked about how Adam was the only child of a family in upper Egypt, how he educated himself and learned to read and write in both Arabic and English, and how he grew up surrounded by temples and historical places that made him fond of the Egyptian history and he mastered the hieroglyphic language.

John looked at Suzan, wondering, "Interesting. Do you know the meaning of his name?"

"You know…Adam… and Sadek, in Arabic, mean Honest!"

He smiled and kept browsing the diary until his eyes stopped on some drawings, and between these drawings was…The sign.

He went back a few pages and started reading out loud, "It was the year 1907 when I met Professor Edward Ayrton, and even with my poor English at that time, we could communicate and talk about the great Pharaohs and Egyptian history. Professor Ayrton believed that the Pharaoh Akhenaten was his next discovery, and when he found my passion for Egyptology, he took me with him. It was a great day when he discovered the mummy, and with it, we found many other things that the Pharaoh was taking to the afterlife based on their beliefs. They were all matching except one thing; it looked like the letter eight but sideways.…"

John stopped reading and looked at his sister. "I told you; it is like an infinity sign, a lazy eight."

She smiled and said, "Just keep reading."

He continued, "However, it wasn't exactly the letter eight, as you can separate it into two parts from the middle. We tried to understand what this tool is for, but we thought it was just artwork or a toy."

John stopped reading and said to his sister, "But the sign was crafted on the mummy's tomb and the statue."

Suzan kept quiet, and John continued reading…

"But then we found this sign crafted on a special part of the tomb, and this symbol is not part of the hieroglyphic language. I think this will be a riddle to solve or just a game from our ancestors to confuse us, as they liked to play games. Or even more, it could be a curse to whoever would disturb the great pharaoh. It must be a spell; otherwise, why are all these nightmares chasing me? And why did Mr. Ayrton drown a few years after the discovery?"

"After the discovery, I moved to England with Professor Ayrton. There, I got married and had a family."

John stopped reading again, "I don't see any other notes about the sign. Also, he didn't mention anything about the statue, so you were right; it is another riddle."

"Not quite a riddle. This diary answers some questions, but we must read it all."

They both turned. Joseph continued talking as he walked downstairs, "Good morning, Mom. Good morning, Uncle John."

"Good morning, Joseph," they answered together.

"So, you heard about your great grandfather's diary. What do you think?" John asked.

Joseph looked at the diary excitedly, "Can I read it?"

"Of course, this is the right time to read it. Your dad never had the passion to read it, and I was always trying to find the time, but it never happened," said Suzan.

"This is a treasure; I will read every page." Joseph seemed dazzled.

John looked happy with his nephew's enthusiasm. "OK, we have formed a team. You will work on the diary. I have a history lesson; Suzan will work on her lab."

"Mmm…A history lesson with Sarah," Suzan sounded skeptical.

"Yes, we will meet today to discuss the museum's report. Let us all meet back here at 5:00 PM. Sounds good?"

They didn't know that it was quite a meeting.

Diary of the Grandfather

"Joseph, your breakfast is on the dining table; don't let it get cold. I will be at the lab; knock on the door or call me if you need anything. We will have lunch together when Uncle John comes back."

Suzan said before heading to the room she had turned into a lab in the basement.

Joseph nodded his head while consumed in the pages of the diary. He took a bite from his sandwich and drank his cup of milk, still turning the pages.

He felt goosebumps when he saw the drawing of the sign and remembered the museum's visit and the drawing on the bathroom mirror. He kept reading the diary until Adam traveled with Prof. Ayrton to England. Adam talked about how life was different in England and how he was so happy back in Egypt.

"My parents loved me so much and did their best to teach me and encourage me to read and learn, and at the same time got me everything I wanted. Now, I need to work to get what I need; I have a family to feed. I love my life here, but I miss Egypt or, more precisely, my childhood in Egypt. One day, I'll go back. It wasn't a metaphor when I said I was chasing my dream, as I was chasing my dream, or was it the other way around, and that dream was chasing me? The dream when I saw this creature with a face you can't describe, a face with no details. I still remember this dream when he pointed to me and said that my fate is to leave this land and follow the stranger who will help me discover who I am!"

Joseph stopped reading and mumbled, "Creature with a face you can't describe..."

"The statue!" he gasped.

He squeezed into the couch, tucking his knees close to his face, and continued reading, "The same dream over and over until I met Prof. Ayrton, and I knew he was the stranger that I have to follow until we discovered the tomb, but then, next to the tomb we found a statue of a creature that you can't identify; it was the same creature who visited me in my dreams. I don't know who and what this thing is, but sometimes, I think it is the devil himself or maybe an angel."

Joseph felt pity for his grandfather and whispered, "Poor Grandpa, why has no one read this diary before? You went through so much! I hope you found peace in the end."

He continued reading the diary to learn more about his grandfather.

London

May 1ˢᵗ, 1935

"I don't have the strength left to write any more precisely. I don't have anything more to write about. I fulfilled everything a man would want in this life, and now it is time to go and pass the baton to the next generation. Now, I will finally be relieved from these dreams that chased me all my life; yesterday was the last dream, as this creature said. Now, I am not sure if those were dreams or if they were real; him actually visiting me! I never told anyone about these visits, so they wouldn't call me crazy, but maybe, one day, this will all make sense. In the last dream, he told me that everything started to change, and soon, I would leave this limited-dimensional world to the multi-dimensional afterlife, and my family would need to leave this land for the promised land. I don't understand what that means, and I don't think I will ever, but I've lost interest in knowledge and the interest of creating a legacy; now is the time to sit back and relax. And as this creature said, *I did my part, and now it is the time for someone else...*"

Joseph turned the last page and kept looking at the papers with a myriad of questions in his mind: How come this creature shows up at different times? Is it the same creature that he saw or something else? What is meant by limited dimensions and multi-dimensions? What happened to Adam after 1935? Does his father know about this? A number of questions were popping into his mind, one after another. But all those questions vanished as his body froze out of fear when he heard a scream coming from the lab.

It was Suzan.

Akhenaten

Sarah walked to the museum's cafeteria, looking for John, who was sitting in the corner, typing the report on his laptop. She sat in front of him, saying, "Looks like it's going to be an interesting report."

"Only because you are helping me write it," he smiled.

"How is Joseph doing?" she smiled back.

"He is doing okay. Thanks. Do you know that his great-grandfather was an Egyptian? And he had the same name as yours…Adam?"

"Adam is a common name all over the world. I think everyone somehow has a family member named Adam."

John looked at her silently before saying, "You're right; now I want to ask you about one of your great grandfathers, the pharaoh Akhenaten. Please tell me more about him. I want to give the readers of the newspaper something exciting, and not just a report about the museum. I want the report to talk more about the pharaoh's life, to create a connection between the reader and the pharaoh."

"Why Him specifically, why not King Tut or Nefertiti or any other Pharaoh from that dynasty?"

"Everyone knows about King Tut; he is the most famous pharaoh in Egyptian history."

Her voice sounded frustrated and a little angry. "Only because they discovered his tomb before it got vandalized, but he was just a kid who wiped out all his dad's revolutionary steps."

John noticed a sudden intenseness in her body, so he smiled and said, "OK, I am not as good as you in history, and I respect your point, but for me, King Tut is not exciting reading material anymore."

"How about Nefertiti?"

"Most readers are overwhelmed with Cleopatra, as she is good reading material, but I think Nefertiti was just a part of the Pharaoh's legacy."

"Oh, my friend, you need to read more about Egyptian history; Nefertiti was behind the Pharaoh's legacy, not just part of it."

"You don't need to give her extra credit just because you look like her," he said with a sneaky smile.

"Is that so? OK, I think you need to look for a different resource for your report then." she acted as if she was standing up to leave, but John held her hand, and they both stood up at the exact moment, leaning forward. Their faces got so close to each other, he didn't even remember how long they had stayed like that, but he did feel her warm breath on his face, and the only thing he saw at that moment was— her eyes. He wished to keep looking at those eyes for the rest of his life. With their faces still close and their lips almost touching, he said, "If Nefertiti had those eyes, then I'm sure she was the pharaoh's ultimate legacy and not just part of it."

"She had the same eyes…" she repeated in a trembling voice.

They slowly sat down again and had this moment of silence, trying to calm down all the feelings rising inside them, before John broke the silence, asking, "OK, I think we'll talk about both of them as a happy family, the pharaoh and his queen. Tell me first about the queen, as they say—ladies first."

She smiled and covered her face with her hands, trying to calm herself down. The intimate moment had passed. She looked at him, pretending to be serious, "We don't know that much about the queen."

He looked at her surprisingly. "Really?! All this lecture about her; why aren't we focusing on the queen?"

"Well, not knowing much about her doesn't mean she didn't play an important role during the pharaoh's era, but we don't know what happened to her after the pharaoh passed away, and we don't know anything about her family, or why the pharaoh chose her to be his queen. She was not from a royal family, and her father was definitely not a priest; no one knows how the love story started between her and the Pharaoh."

"What about Akhenaten?"

"He was a rebel," she said after a deep breath.

"What do you mean?"

"Changing his name from Amenhotep, the fourth, who followed the Amen temple to Akhenaten, who followed the God Aten, challenging all the priests and destroying their legacy and the theocracy that was controlling the country for ages, abandoning the idea of polytheism and promoting the idea of one God that was represented by the sun as that was the first monotheistic religion, to the point a lot of Egyptologists are thinking that he is more as a Prophet, not a pharaoh; he changed the capital from Thebes to a new city that is now known as Amarna, and also changed the designs of the temples completely different from the old fashioned temples to a new style of architecture."

She continued in a passionate voice, "Choosing a regular girl and making her his wife, then putting her next to him in every drawing; what else do you call him if not a rebel?"

"If we are not talking about someone who lived more than three thousand years ago, I would say you love him."

She was still consumed in her thoughts. "More than three thousand years, and it still feels like yesterday…"

She stopped jabbering, but John looked at her perplexed expression. "Feel like yesterday…What do you mean?"

She could change the subject easily or come up with anything, but she added another parameter to the equation. After leaving Jacob's office, she wanted to help John as planned.

She pressed his hands and looked straight into his eyes.

"John, you need to break the code and read the message, use the sign, and you will find all the answers."

Then, she walked away, but right before she left, she turned and walked back to him, held his face, and kissed him for a second, a kiss that made him feel—alive. She then stepped back and said, "I missed you." She continued, "Read Adam's diary carefully; it will help you and Suzan solve this riddle."

John's jaw dropped, as he was totally confused between the surprising kiss and what Sarah said *that she missed him*, and then how did she know about Suzan? His doubts about Sarah were now becoming facts, as he was sure that she was not just an Egyptologist he met by chance at the museum, but she was someone way more than that, more than he ever imagined!

Intruders

Suzan walked to her lab with David's notes and a million thoughts in her mind. She set up the microscope on her office desk, and the first thing she did was to connect it with the camera installed in David's throat, but the camera was offline.

She mumbled, "How come it is offline? Did David destroy it before sending me the video? Even if he extracted it, I could still see it…"

She sighed, switched the microscope to her camera, and set a video record to trigger and track any activity of any foreign items, but everything looked clear, as if she was never infected.

She started searching the laptop for any videos, but there were none saved, which raised her suspicions that there should be some saved videos of all the research that David was working on. She started to check the notes, all everyday notes she already knew from the previous work together. She closed the notebook and smiled, "Oh, David, you are an old-school scientist who still writes his notes in a 70-sheet notebook."

She looked at the notebook and mumbled, "Except this one is way lighter than 70 pages. She opened it again and started exploring the pages many times before saying in a low voice, "Only 60 sheets; what happened to these ten pages, David? What did you find out and write on these pages? And why did you keep it a secret, unless…"

She paused for a second before continuing, "Unless someone took those papers from the notebook, why didn't they take it all? Why did they leave the notebook behind, and who are they, and what did they do to you, poor David???"

She felt her head would explode from all these thoughts, so she put her head between her hands and closed her eyes to clear her mind.

All the thoughts started to flow in her mind, from Terry's affair until John's visit and Joseph's journey to the museum, and then David's experiment and his last video message, "Suzan… it is coming after you…"

She suddenly left her head and moved the chair to her computer and typed some codes, then went back to the microscope and typed some instructions until she got a confirmation message, "New location saved." And then, the screen switched to a different view. She sat back, kept her eyes wide open, and said, "Now we wait and see if I'm crazy or I'm actually about to discover something crazy!"

It took ten minutes looking before her eyes got even wider, seeing what was happening on the screen. She zoomed the view to the maximum, and her jaw dropped; her eyes almost left her face looking at the screen before she jumped from the chair screaming, "BINGO."

She screamed so loud that Joseph knocked at the door. Before she opened, he ran inside, hugging her and breathing heavily. "Mom, are you OK?"

She hugged him tightly and held his face between her hands, and in an excited voice, she said, "I'm Okay, I'm Okay."

Before Joseph could say more, she continued with the same excitement, "Did you read your grandfather's diary?"

Joseph nodded, "Yes, it is scary and confusing, Mom. I need to go through it again."

"OK, you keep working on your part, and I will work here until Uncle John comes back, but first, I need to do something." Suzan patted his cheek.

She took an injection loaded with the last nano-camera and looked at Joseph, saying, "I need to make sure you are doing okay. We will try this injection, and I promise it won't hurt."

"I trust you, Mom."

She smiled and gently pressed the injection on his neck and looked closely at the monitor to see the camera moving at Joseph's throat. It started sending life images. She said, "OK, you go do your part, and I'll do mine."

Joseph nodded with a smile and closed the door behind him.

Suzan looked at the microscope's screen, "Hello visitors, let's find out who you are."

She looked closely at the video on her camera. She zoomed it into the maximum to see the virus that started showing on the monitor, but not as packs but one by one, going to the exact same location and staying there for seconds before disappearing, and then another one showing up. She captured one image from the video that showed the virus and sent it to her laptop. She processed the image using another computer program, magnified it multiple times, and looked at the screen, waiting for a final resolution. Her eyes got stuck to the screen in front of her, and she said in a scared and trembling voice, "Oh my God, David was right; this is not just a virus. These are…"

The doorbell interrupted her self-talk. She heard Joseph from outside, running to open the door.

"Hello Michael, Come in."

Michael

"Hello, Joseph, how are you? Did you practice your lessons?" Michael asked while taking off his Jacket and putting it aside.

Michael was teaching Joseph music and martial arts. When Suzan discovered Joseph's passion for music, she requested that her neighbor teach him piano. Michael also recommended martial arts to help him meditate and control his feelings. Still, because Joseph was not feeling up to it among groups and found it difficult to blend in, private lessons were the optimal solution. As a result, Joseph made significant progress on focusing better and emotional control.

Michael was a young, athletic man in his early thirties—handsome—quiet—polite—and strong. He studied Music and Martial Arts for several years and read a lot, particularly about the universe, space, and physics. Besides all that, he was great with children, especially with Joseph. He had built a connection with him in no time. Most of the time, they talked about different subjects apart from music and martial arts. Michael had become Joseph's mentor and friend at the same time.

Suzan went outside to welcome Michael and fix him coffee while Joseph walked to the Piano and sat there. He started playing some notes when Michael sat next to him, listening. He looked at him and said, "You look distracted, Joseph, is everything OK?"

"I'm okay, sorry. I was thinking about something else, but I'll now focus on the lesson."

"You don't need to focus on the music; just play, and Music will take you away naturally, and that will eventually clear your mind and help you to focus—music is the tool, not the goal."

Joseph looked at Michael and asked, "You really love music, don't you? I can see that when you play, it's like you are not here anymore, you are…" Joseph felt stuck in words.

Michael smiled, "Like I am out of this world, free from this limited dimensional world to the open universe!"

Joseph's eyes went wide open as he felt a sense of awe and wonder; they were the exact words that Adam had used in his diary, so he looked at Michael and, in a deep voice, asked him, "What do you mean by limited dimensional world?"

Michael smiled as he looked at Joseph and responded, "OK, I meant that music would take you away and…"

Joseph interrupted him, "No, what did you literally mean by limited dimensional world?" He went further to explain as he saw the question and confusion in Michael's eyes. "Sorry, I was reading my great-grandfather's diary, and he used the same expression, so I was wondering, what does it really mean?"

"Oh, that's awesome. Did your grandfather play music?"

"I don't think so; he never mentioned music in his notes."

Michael looked at Joseph and said, "OK, I am not sure what the context was where he mentioned this sentence, so I will try to explain the idea of multi-dimensions to you, although you may be too young to understand. Let's drop the music today as it takes us out of this universe and actually speak about the Universe."

He said that while picking a piece of paper in front of him and said, "If we draw a line on this paper, we call this line one dimensional, and this dimension is called length, correct?"

Joseph nodded.

Michael smiled and continued, "OK, look at this paper. It has length and width, which we call two dimensions. Are you following, Joseph?"

Joseph nodded. "Yes, and I see where this is going, the three dimensions, like this piano, as it has length, width, and height."

Michael smiled and proudly said, "I knew you were a smart kid. Now, things will get more interesting—how about the fourth dimension?"

Joseph sounded excited, "I know it; the fourth dimension is time."

Michael smiled, "Mmm…. Yes and no, let me explain. Do you know Albert Einstein?"

Joseph, with excitement, nodded yes.

Michael continued, "According to Albert Einstein and Mostafa Musharraf, time is a dimension like the other three dimensions, and if we manage to move with the ultimate speed in the universe, and that is the speed of light, then we can move through the time back and forth. This is part of the relativity theory and the special relativity theory, something you will enjoy reading about and maybe study in High school, but what if…" Michael paused and looked at Joseph.

Joseph looked overwhelmed, "What if what?"

"What if there is an actual fourth dimension, a dimension that we can't see and can't feel?"

Michael's voice became softer and deeper. Joseph was paying attention.

"Look at this paper and think of it as a two-dimensional world, as it only has length and width, no height, and no up or down. All creatures on this paper can only move left or right on the length and width; they don't understand what is up or down as it is beyond their knowledge and imagination. So, do you think these creatures on this two-dimensional world paper will ever know we existed?"

Joseph looked a little confused, then he paused a little more before answering, "No, they will never know that we exist as they can't see us."

"Unless we somehow entered this world!" Suzan said that with a concerned voice while pulling a chair to sit next to them. "Sorry, would you mind if I joined? This is an interesting subject."

Michael waved his hand, welcoming her. "Sure, you said exactly what I was about to say."

"As you said, Joseph, they will never know that we exist unless, somehow, we can enter their two-dimensional world, but before we do that, we need to have the ability, energy, and imagination to think about this two-dimensional world. Think about it again, Joseph, a world with only length and height…"

Joseph is now feeling anxious. "I would never have thought about it until you mentioned it."

Michael's smile was reassuring. "Now, before we continue, I want you to hold this pencil and put a point on the lower part of the paper and tell me how this point, we assume is a creature living on this paper, will move up to the other edge of the paper?"

Joseph draws the point, then says, "OK, it needs to move on the length dimension and then to the width dimension to reach the other corner."

Michael made a clapping gesture. "Yes, exactly! And to do that, it will take a very long time."

Then he looked at Joseph's eyes, held the paper in front of his face, and said, "But what if we bend the paper to make our point reach its destination?"

Suzan interrupted, "Now you used the height, which is an unknown dimension to that world, to make that point travel through...."

Joseph continued with excitement, "Time!"

Michael laughed out loud and looked at Joseph. "You are the smartest kid ever."

Then he continued, "Take this rule and apply it to any universe, as always—the next dimension is time, so, for the two-world dimension, the third dimension is time, but for us, it is height, and the fourth dimension is time, but for a four-dimensional world, it is just a dimension like length, width, and height. You see what I mean?"

Joseph was swamped and astonished with all this information, and Suzan was smiling as what Michael said explained most of her concerns.

Then, Michael took the pencil and held the paper with the other hand before continuing, "Now, let's assume that this pencil from the three-dimensional world had decided to go through this paper..."

He said that while moving the pencil closer to the paper, the light started showing a shadow of a point on the paper. He then started flipping the pencil to convert the shadow to a line.

"Now, the shape of the pencil on the paper depends on the angle of this pencil when it interacts with the paper, and all creatures on this paper will never see a pencil. They will only see what their world allows them to see. So, if the pencil were perpendicular, they would only see a dot; if the pencil were horizontal, it would look like a line; if this was a cube, and it's entering this paper, it will..."

Joseph interrupted excitedly, "It will look like a square!"

Michael laughed, and Suzan felt proud of her son. Michael said, "Exactly, yes, it would look like a square if it landed flat, or it would look like a triangle if it landed with an angle, but now you understand the concept."

"Now, I need your full attention, Joseph. As we agreed, these creatures on the two world dimensions can't see what is above, so they will never see the pencil until it actually touches the paper, and for them, this pencil appeared suddenly out of nowhere. It will disappear suddenly into thin air when it leaves the paper. If this pencil stayed on the paper, they would never know what it actually looks like as it is beyond their ability to see the three dimensions. So for these creatures, this pencil is a time traveler, and for this world of two-dimensional paper, the third dimension is not height, but as we said before, it is time."

Suzan was astonished; she looked at Michael and said, "Let me repeat that to make sure we understand correctly. Do you mean that the fourth dimension in our world is just another dimension, and there could be a whole universe we don't see?"

Michael nodded and continued, "Yes, until the creatures from this fourth-dimensional world have the knowledge and energy to see us and then decide to interact with us, and in that case, they will show up and disappear, moving freely on that unknown dimension that we call time."

Suzan asked, "But what about the pencil's shadow on the paper? The two-dimensional world creatures can see the pencil's shadow before it interacts with the paper, right?"

Michael nodded, moved the paper to a dark corner, and got the pencil closer to the paper. He then looked at Suzan and said, "What about now? How the shadow appears is based on the pencil's decision on how and when to enter the paper world, as when it is dark or light also depends on the speed of the pencil going through the paper, even if the creatures on that paper notice the shadow, they won't be able to interact with it, because it is a shadow of undefined shape; so they

86

can't touch it or capture it until the pencil actually interacts with the paper."

Joseph was silent for a moment and then muttered, "The Statue."

Michael looked at him, wondering, "What Statue?"

Suzan quickly responded, "This is a story Joseph and I were reading, and some creatures were showing and disappearing."

Michael nodded.

"This theory about multidimensional universes could explain all the paranormal activity when you see things appear and disappear. Also, seeing things that look weird and undefined, as we call them ghosts or whatever, is because they entered our world at a certain angle before it took the shape of something familiar that our eyes can understand."

Joseph said, "Like the statue."

Michael smiled at him, "You really like this story; I am intrigued to read it."

Suzan interrupted again, "But all these are just theories, and nothing has been proved. Besides, doesn't that make our world vulnerable to a higher dimensional world?"

"This theory is part of what is called superstring theory, but this is the thing about physics; it all starts with theories, and then science will prove it right or wrong. I don't think we are vulnerable to a higher dimension, as our world could only be noticeable by the fourth-dimensional world, i.e., if they care about primitive creatures like us, or if they think it is worth it to communicate with us or if they even know that we exist, especially it takes a lot of energy to travel between a different dimensional universe. This energy could affect our fourth dimension, our time, and in the end, they want to keep us safe, as their universe is based on ours."

"What do you mean?" it was Suzan's turn to be confused.

Michael looked at Joseph and smiled. "OK, I will let Joseph answer this question. If you put cubes on top of each other and suddenly pull the third cube, what will happen to the other cubes?"

"All the cubes above the third cube will fall."

Michael smiled and looked at Suzan. "Exactly, if we fall, then everything above us will fall. So, if creatures with four dimensions contact us, they will care about our existence, as their existence depends on us. That is why they will be cautious with the energy they use to go through dimensions to enter our world, or otherwise they will risk their lives."

Suzan nodded, "So these four-dimensional creatures can see and destroy or control us, so they are like God?"

Michael laughed. "God! Oh, God is way more than that. The superstring theory discusses a ten-dimensional universe; if true, God is on the eleventh dimension. God is way more than any dimension."

Suzan agreed, "You're right; based on this theory, the universe is like a ten-story building!"

"Remember, this is still a theory, and there is another version of it assuming the universe is twenty-two dimensional, but what I believe is that, if the Universe is a multistory building, it is not just ten or twenty stories."

He paused briefly and then said with a mysterious smile on his face, "It would be a skyscraper."

Suzan looked at Michael and said in a genuine tone, "I am really glad I joined you guys in this interesting conversation; what do you think, Joseph?"

Joseph smiled and looked at Michael. "I love you, Michael. Thank you for being you."

Michael gave Joseph a warm hug, then looked at him and said, "I love you back, Joseph, and I really think you are a very smart kid. Who knows, I'm sure you will make this world a better place one day, but for now, I will take your leave and see you next week."

With that said, he took his jacket and went to the door, then turned back to Joseph and asked, "What was the name of that book you were reading? It sounded like an interesting story."

Joseph smiled and said, "It is more like a book I am writing; I am thinking of naming it "The Quiz.""

Michael smiled and winked at him, saying, "I like it."

Joseph and Suzan thought of the same thing; they had more answers now and must share them with John ASAP.

The Code

John sat at the dining table, looking at Joseph and Suzan. He wiped his face with his palms, trying to keep his mind focused.

"So, your piano teacher had a theory that could explain all this mess we are dealing with?!!"

Joseph replied, "It is not his theory, but he's reading a lot about it, and it is called Superstring theory." Then, his voice turned slightly sarcastic. "As we explained to you more than three times, based on this theory, we might face creatures from another dimension."

"Creatures from another dimension?!"

He looked at Suzan. "Hey, the only thing we saw was that statue, and all of these events just started yesterday, so what creatures are we talking about?" John said in a denial tone.

Suzan looked at John and then looked at Joseph before looking back at John. She took a deep breath and said in a fearful and concerned voice, "The creatures that live inside us, John, the creatures that we thought for a long time were a different strain of the virus."

John looked at her, still confused. "We thought it was a virus; if not, what is it?"

She tried to hide her fear and sound calm but couldn't. She looked straight into his eyes and said, "Drones."

John was perplexed over his sister explaining her theory, and so was Joseph, trying to understand what his mother was trying to explain.

After almost half an hour, John stood up, went to the kitchen, and returned with a cup of coffee and a big glass of milk in a few minutes. Before sitting down, he handed the milk to Joseph.

"I think you need this."

Joseph smiled, "Indeed."

John took a big sip of his coffee before looking at Suzan. He said, "OK, repeat what you said."

Suzan smiled and took a piece of paper and a pencil. She started to explain what she found in the lab.

"As you know, we were dealing with a virus that has all the symptoms of flu, but it is more aggressive and is causing severe lung damage. Also, in some cases, it could cause a heart attack."

She stopped talking to ensure they followed; John and Joseph nodded, and Suzan continued drawing a simple figure of a human body on paper, pointing to the throat and the lungs.

"All our research focused on those two areas, where the virus could incubate, but we never understood how some cases could also have a heart attack. In some cases, they lose vision or get paralyzed, and how is the virus behaving differently with no pattern of its life expectancy, as that is not normal. The virus must have a life expectancy, then die. With this kind of virus, it can't stay alive for more than two weeks, but in some cases, we kept seeing activity for months."

She took a deep breath, and her voice went down as she remembered David. She continued, "Until David decided to use the nano-cameras and shared his experiments with me, and then he disappeared, as you know, John."

She said that, looking at John and pressing her words, because she did not want Joseph to get terrified about what happened to David.

John nodded with a subtle smile as he understood what his sister wanted while Joseph drank his milk and focused on what his mom was explaining.

"When I was checking David's notes, ten pages were missing; it looks like someone didn't want us to find those pages, but at the same time, they left all the other notes as they were. Apparently, they wanted us to continue the research."

John interrupted her, "Who are they?"

Joseph answered, "Whoever put those drones inside our bodies."

Suzan smiled at Joseph and continued, "I had to think like David, whatever happened in the lab, and how this virus appears and disappears. First, David's experiment, and then you brought me David's notes, and because of you, John, I had an idea."

John asked in a surprised whisper, "Idea, what idea?"

Suzan smiled and said, "Remember when you told me the only way to defeat the enemy within you is to clear your mind and step back to see the big picture?"

Still confused, John said, "Yes, I remember, but what does that have to do with the virus?"

She continued as if she did not hear him, "I decided to step back and look at the big picture, and then, I had this crazy idea!"

John and Joseph both had question marks on their faces.

She continued, "If the behavior of this virus is different, then why do we insist that it is a virus? Why didn't we think that it is something else that can decide when to appear and when to disappear, something that can decide the fate of the incubating body based on the data they collect?"

John looked at her, "You mean?"

Joseph nodded instead. "Yes, Uncle John, she means exactly what you're thinking...Robots!"

Suzan nodded, too. "Yes, nanobots, to be more precise, rather nano drones, can collect data and transmit it to somewhere else. Also, they can see and hear what we see and hear and react based on that. We are talking about high technology that is either a secret or is not from this earth."

"This is all hypothesis…" John was still feeling doubtful.

She interrupted him, "That was the only assumption that explains how this thing appears and disappears. When I removed the mask, it was like it could see what we were doing, and they were communicating when two incubator bodies were in close range without wearing a mask, but again, I listened to what you said and looked at the big picture."

This time, Joseph pointed to a certain point on the paper. "Yes, Mom, you let the nano camera look here."

She smiled and nodded, feeling proud of her son while John was still confused. "Why here?"

She looked at him and said, "Because I had to look at the big picture, and if my assumption is right about those drones, then they will need power, and the power station in the body will be the magical sinoatrial node located in the…"

Joseph kept pointing to the same spot while looking at John. "The Heart."

John started to digest the idea but was still a bit confused. "But why is it going to this node?"

"Because this node produces 0.9 volts that will cause the heart to beat and with the right receptors and amplifications on those drones, they can charge their nanobatteries by using this voltage, and that is why in some cases, were not able to handle this charging process, and their sinoatrial node failed, after which, they suffered a heart attack."

She took a large picture from the bag beside her and continued, "After a little bit, the camera captured those drones on the node without the nanobots' Como flash. I could see it clearly for the first time after I used the maximum magnification on the camera." She put the picture on the table that showed a drone with a clear label on one of the sides, a tag that looked like an infinity symbol."

John paused at the picture, then looked at them, saying, "Everything is connected strangely; it's like someone is connecting all these dots: the virus, the sign, the museum, the superstring theory, the diary, and then Sarah."

Suzan smiled and asked, "Didn't you tell us what happened with Sarah?"

He looked at them and said, "I thought you'd think I was crazy if I told you what I found, but I'm guessing that after all that we found, there is nothing crazy anymore."

Joseph finished his last sip of milk and said, "I agree; more crazy things are happening, and what is crazy is that they all seem normal now. So, what happened with Sarah?"

John told them about all that happened but avoided the kissing part for some reason.

Suzan asked him confusedly, "How could she know about Adam's diary?"

Joseph was silent and looked like he was thinking about something. He looked at them and pressed his words as he said, "She knows because Sarah and Nefertiti are the same person!"

Suzan looked at him and said, "As you said, nothing is crazy anymore, but I think this is a little bit crazier; how come Sarah and Nefertiti are the same person with a difference of more than three thousand years between them?"

Joseph responded with a smile, "Remember, time is just a dimension?"

John interrupted, "Not for us; it is a dimension for four-dimensional creatures from a four-dimensional universe."

He stopped talking for a moment and then said, "Unless you mean…"

Joseph nodded. "Yes, Uncle John, Sarah is neither a human nor Nefertiti."

Suzan took a deep breath. "I think the only way is to listen to what Sarah said."

"What do you mean?" John asked.

"We need to reread the diary and break the code. This is the only way to solve this mystery," said Joseph.

Then he continued, "I know who can help us with the code."

Suzan smiled. "You mean Fatima?"

Joseph nodded as yes, and looking at John, he said, "Yes, she is my friend and a computer genius. Also, Isaac, who is very smart and passionate about Egyptology."

Suzan sounded excited. "They both live in the neighborhood. I can invite them both for dinner, and we can all talk. I trust both kids; they always play with Joseph and are super nice together."

"OK, invite them here so we can talk, but don't share any details with them until we all sit and talk. No one should know anything yet."

He thought of something and asked, "Suzan, you said those drones can hear us and see what we see, right? This means…"

Suzan interrupted in a calm voice, "Yes, John, this means they heard everything we said now, and there is no way to avoid that."

Looking at John's worried face, she continued in a calmer voice.

"But for some reason, I am not worried about that."

She drew the sign on the paper and said, "We should now focus only on breaking the code."

Afreet

Dr. Jacob opened the door of his house, located in the suburbs of Los Angeles, and walked in with steady steps before he stopped. His sharp eyes looked around. He smiled and said, "You are consuming energy for no reason; I can sense you standing at this corner."

He pointed at one corner of the living room, and from that corner, the statue's shape started to show up, which then transformed into a human form.

Jacob looked at him and walked to a couch in the middle of the living room. He pointed towards a fridge on the other corner, saying, "Help yourself with a drink if you like."

The creature looked at him and, in a deep voice, said, "I don't need to pretend and act like those primitives."

Jacob smiled again and gestured to him to sit down while he walked to the fridge and got himself a drink. Taking a big gulp of his drink, he looked at the creature, saying, "But I like to act like them; you know that we do count on them to finish this mission, so in the end, they are not that primitive."

The creature nodded, saying, "I know we count on them."

Jacob's face turned red, and he screamed, "If you know that, so what the heck were you thinking killing three major players!"

The creature ignored his question and anger and calmly looked at him, asking, "Where is Sarah?"

Jacob's voice surprisingly turned calm again, like he wasn't screaming a second ago. He said, "I had to send her back; she didn't follow the rules… again."

The creature smiled. "Yes, again!"

Then he sat straight and looked at Jacob's eyes, "She always has and will always break the rules!"

Jacob kept eye contact; this time, he ignored the creature's comment and calmly asked him, "Why did you kill them?"

"You know that I had to kill David. He acted differently than planned, and you know the consequences of uncalculated actions."

Still, calm and maintaining eye contact, Jacob said, "I know the consequences, but I also know that we shouldn't interrupt any action; that was the agreement."

The creature interrupted him this time, shouting, "Screw this agreement, we can't handle more traffic, we can't handle dealing with more parameters, I had to put things back on track!"

"But you already created more parameters and increased the traffic by killing him," said Jacob.

The creature leaned forward and whispered, "But I cleaned the mess!"

In the same calm tone, Jacob said, "By killing more people?"

"Yes, Jacob, by killing more people, I had to kill Terry to get things back on balance. You know what Terry and David were supposed to do together, and by taking David out of the equation, I had to take out Terry as well, which put things back on track as we already had the replacement."

Jacob leaned forward, crossing his fingers in front of his face, and paused for a second as he was thinking about what he heard before leaning back on the couch, and, in a concerned voice, said, "You are doing the right things in a wrong way, that will never work and if they figured out, we would lose the whole game."

The creature smiled, looking like a vicious snake. "They will never figure out because they never existed."

Jacob crossed his thick eyebrows and paused for a second before he laughed out loud and, between his laugh, said, "That is why you killed Laura! But how did you know?"

The creature smiled, "I spent my time studying; their whole universe was based on Laura getting married to John, and then in different time zones, they would have a child who would cause all this mess, and the story continues. They were arrogant and ignorant; they didn't know their existence depended on that incident. I convinced them that I would be a double agent and kill Laura to save their universe from the ultimate fate, and I got everyone's approval also, so if things went wrong, no one would blame us. I also told them you are an old-school type; hence, it's better not to tell you about the agreement. Those stupid Afreets didn't study or read; they only looked under their feet and thought this would give them an advantage over everyone else. Thus, they agreed."

After he stopped laughing, Jacob looked at him, saying, "They didn't follow the rules, and they…"

The creature continued, "Vanished as they never existed, and now the traffic is way lighter, and the task is way easier."

Jacob could not hide his admiration for what the creature did, then he said. "That is why you stayed behind on that day we had the meeting?"

Then he looked more concerned now and said, "Listen, they vanished because they looked for a quick victory and played against the rules, and this is exactly what you are doing now. The same situation a long time ago caused all this to happen after we lived in peace for ages, longer than I remember, until Sarah played against the rules."

The creature looked at Jacob, and he sounded like a crazy scientist who had discovered his greatest invention. "What Sarah did was stupid at that time, but it was the reason to give us the power and the reason we had the knowledge that others never had. Besides, it was the reason to name our race, remember?"

Jacob smiled, and he looked like he remembered something that happened a long time ago. "Yes, I remember when she came back telling us that she was spotted, and the human who spotted her called her Afreet." His smile widened as he continued, "We found the name powerful, especially because it means *creature with supernatural power* in the human language at that time, so we proposed the name to the council to be our race name, and since then, we are Afreets."

The creature smiled. "Yes, I remember, but I needed you to remember our existence, our knowledge, and our survival, all because of a naive action from an amateur who didn't follow the rules, but in that time, we had the tolerance to accept mistakes, and we worked on fixing it."

Jacob nodded before saying, "Not anymore; time is running, and with great responsibilities, there is no more room for mistakes. You didn't check the traffic in the last hour; after you killed Laura, the traffic got lighter by more than 50%, but after Sarah talked to John, the traffic was 150%. We have less than 24 hours to fix that roadblock. Otherwise, it is not just our existence but everyone's existence."

The creature looked scared for the first time. "What do you mean by everyone?"

Jacob pressed his words in a firm voice, "I mean, we need to recalculate all actions and act accordingly. After 24 hours, it is either our victory day or..."

He paused for a second, "Or it is doomsday."

Fatima & Isaac

Los Angeles - California

Thursday March 6th, 2025

Time 6:00 PM

Suzan rang the bell of her neighbor's house. A middle-aged Woman with a headscarf opened the door with a big smile. "Hey Suzan, Hello Joseph, Hello Isaac."

A loud laughter from inside was heard. Fatima was running from inside when she heard her mom saying Joseph and Isaac's names. She ran to the front door. With a big smile on her baby face and a wide, exciting eye behind her glasses, she asked, "Hey guys, what are you doing here?"

Her mom gave her a stern look. "Fatima, this is rude. First, you have to invite your friends inside. Come on, Suzan, we were about to have dinner; join us."

Suzan smiled. "Thanks, Salma, I can't resist the delicious aroma wafting from your kitchen, but I wanted to ask if Fatima can join Joseph and Isaac for dinner at my house? My brother John is visiting and working on a report about the Egyptian exhibition here in Los Angeles. Isaac and Fatima are passionate about Egyptian history, so I thought it would be fun if they could join us over dinner while we talk about John's report."

"Please, Mom, please let me go. I am done with my homework."

Salma smiled and nodded. "OK, but first, let me give you some Syrian Kunafah I baked today."

Isaac handed Salma a plate of babka, saying, "My mom asked me to give this to you."

Salma smiled. "Rachel is the best; I love to eat babka with hot tea. Do you want some Suzan?"

Suzan smiled and said, "Thank you. Rachel also gave me a plate; it will be a feast between your Kunafah and her Babka."

Then, looking at Fatima, she continued, "Bring your laptop in case you want to do some research while John is talking to you about the exhibition."

Fatima ran inside, returned with her laptop, and walked with John and Isaac.

Suzan addressed Salma, "I will bring her back around 9:00 PM."

On the way to Suzan's house, Fatima looked at Joseph and asked, "What is going on? I am not buying the exhibition story!"

Isaac replied, "Neither do I, but Joseph said his uncle would explain everything."

He said that while walking inside Suzan's house, Joseph led them to the dining room, where there was pizza on the table, and John was smiling.

Suzan gestured, inviting them, "I made sure this Pizza is Kosher; I know you both don't eat ham or pork."

Fatima and Isaac nodded in affirmative. With a big smile, they sat at the table, and the three of them started digging at the pizza while John looked at the two plates Suzan brought to the table. "What is that?" he asked.

Suzan smiled. "That's a lot of calories from our neighbors, Kunafah and Babka."

John smiled and patted his belly. "We definitely need some sugar." He started digging into both plates, cheering on how yummy they tasted while the three kids laughed out loud as Suzan fixed tea and milk for everyone.

After dinner, they all sat around the table. Joseph brought the 3D print of the inscription and another 3D of the coffin as Suzan printed it from the photos that John took at the museum. At the same time, Joseph got his grandfather's diary, and they put everything in the middle of the table.

Both Isaac and Fatima seemed clueless about what was going on. John looked at them and wondered how these three 10-year-old kids could help solve this puzzle! Isaac looked sharp and intelligent with wide black eyes, broad forehead, curly black hair, and light brown skin, while Fatima had long light brown hair and rounded glasses that couldn't hide her sharp, smart brown eyes. She had this cute smile on her baby face all the time. She was the one who broke the silence as she fixed her glasses on her nose and looked at John, saying, "We can't start this mission by you doubting our skills!"

John looked at her and smiled. "If I doubted your skills, you wouldn't be here now."

She gave him an exacting glance before switching on her laptop and said, "Good, now what is going on?"

Isaac was focusing on the items over the table before he looked at Fatima and said, "They want you to break the code of this inscription so they can read a hidden message on that coffin."

Joseph looked at his grandfather's diary, and John and Suzan were surprised how Isaac figured out the task before anyone even talked about it."

John looked at Joseph and said, "Joseph, I thought we agreed not to…"

Isaac interrupted John and said, "Joseph didn't tell me anything yet, but it was obvious you guys want us for something, and by looking at all these 3D prints, as I can read the heliographic language, I can tell that this inscription is written with a secret code, especially with this repeating infinity sign. Then having Fatima here means you want someone good with computers and algorithms to break that code, so you need someone like me to read it for you, and you want all of that to be done in secret! You can't trust anyone except Joseph's close friends."

Joseph smiled while talking to John with his eyes still on the diary. "I told you, Uncle John, this team will break the code."

John was still surprised and was about to say something, but he got even more surprised when Fatima looked at them and said, "OK, I took a few pictures of the inscription while Isaac was bragging about his analytical skills, and I can build an algorithm to break that code."

Both Suzan and John looked at each other before looking back at those ten-year-olds. Fatima was typing super-fast on her computer.

"We need to get this done before my bedtime; then you guys can tell me later what it was all about," she said.

Isaac was reading the drawings on the coffin, writing notes on paper, and searching on his laptop, while Joseph was consumed by his grandfather's notes, trying to find a clue that could help them break the code.

Fatima was focusing on the algorithm on her laptop and mumbled, "Something is wrong about this algorithm; this infinity sign is…"

Joseph interrupted her while reading his grandfather's notes, "It's not an infinity sign; it's two alpha signs connected."

Fatima looked at him with a surprised look. "Seriously, why didn't you say that earlier?"

She said she needed to fix the code while typing on her laptop. Joseph looked confused, holding the paper that had the drawings from the diary. Then he looked towards his mom and asked, "Mom, why is each paper wrapped in plastic?"

Suzan looked at him. "The papers were almost 100 years old, and I didn't want them to get ruined."

Joseph was focusing on holding the paper with the drawings. "This paper feels heavier and thicker than the other papers; I'll unwrap it," he said while bringing a pair of scissors. He carefully cut the edges to take out the paper from the plastic. Suddenly, his eyes glowed with a smile of victory. He said, "I knew it."

He cautiously pulled the edge of the paper to find another piece sticking to the back of the paper with the drawing.

Suzan gasped and said, "I must have mistakenly put the two papers in one plastic wrap."

On the other paper, there were only a few lines, and on the top, Adam had written; (The Dream).

The Dream

'It was not like the other dreams with this weird-looking Afreet. Unlike those scary dreams, this one was so peaceful; I was standing in the middle of nowhere when I saw him coming towards me. I felt I knew him, but at the same time, I still couldn't see what he looked like; I couldn't recognize the details of his face, but I felt okay getting closer to him; he handed me this cup of water, it was a strange cup as it looked exactly like this weird sign that we found in the tomb. Then he got very close to me, and his hand pointed to the cup. He was asking me to look inside. I looked inside the cup to see his face, but this time, I could recognize a smile on his face, a very peaceful smile. Then, I took a sip of the water. It was delicious, and I was very thirsty, so I drank all of it. After that, he disappeared, and I woke up. I never saw him again, but my other scary visitor kept visiting me, over and over.'

Joseph finished reading the paper. They were all looking at each other. John and Suzan seemed disappointed; Fatima and Joseph focused on the document while Isaac looked at the inscription.

John asked in a frustrated voice, "That's it, nothing else?"

Suzan paused and raised her hand as she figured something, but then, she put her hand down again and said, "Maybe there is another hidden page?"

Both of them started carefully checking every page, unwrapping the plastic covers to make sure there weren't any more pages they missed and did not read.

Joseph muttered, "I read the diary; if there is anything pointing to the inscription, then it must be this page."

Isaac smiled and looked at John. "You don't need to unwrap the rest of the papers; the answer to our question was on that paper," he said as he pointed at the paper that described the dream.

He picked up his phone and took some photos of the inscription. Then he did something on the pictures and looked at Fatima, "Please upload these new photos to your algorithm."

Fatima looked at the photos and nodded while Joseph looked at them. He felt excited. "Isaac, you are a genius!"

John and Suzan were clueless about what was going on, but then Isaac looked at them with a smile and said, "OK, let me explain while Fatima is doing her coding magic."

Then he looked at them and said, "Read the page again, and you will find this visitor handed him the cup of water. Adam was thirsty, as we are all thirsty for knowledge to break the code. He never figured out what this visitor looked like, but he could only see a smile in his reflection in the water. So, this vague inscription would be clearer if we looked at its reflection. That is why I took more photos and added mirror effects, left to right and up to down, and guess what? The only thing that stayed the same after the mirror effect was the infinity sign, as it is the cup that holds the truth."

Joseph looked so proud of his friends and was about to say something, but Fatima spoke before him. "Good Job, Isaac. I must go now before my mother gets upset."

"How about the algorithm? Could you stay a little bit longer?" Suzan asked.

Fatima smiled and looked at Joseph. "Check your email. I broke the code and sent you a program that reads different kinds of Holographic language," she said while packing her laptop.

Suzan stood up to walk Isaac and Fatima to their home while Joseph switched on his laptop. John was still surprised about what just happened between those three kids. He asked Fatima, "Aren't you interested in knowing what is written there?"

Fatima smiled back at John, "I am more interested in the future and what will happen. I have a test tomorrow and don't want to miss it."

For a reason, John felt shiver about what she said, as he was worried about what could happen tomorrow, but then he smiled and said, "A smart kid like you will never miss a test."

He felt happy watching Joseph leave his laptop and walk with his friends to the door.

I heard him saying to Isaac and Fatima, "You know, guys, we are a great team when we work together."

They nodded and headed out.

John looked at the laptop and decided to keep himself busy until Joseph came back, so he started digging into both the Kunafah and the Babka.

The council

Place: Unknown

Date: Undefined

Time: Doesn't Exist

Jacob walked through the door to a huge hall that looked like a presidential palace. The walls had three-dimensional photos of galaxies, solar systems, mountains, and rivers. There were other photos of people in different places like parks and streets. The images looked so real since they were in motion as if they were open windows to actual events. You could see fish, all kinds of Sea World creatures swimming in the rivers and oceans, and all types of animals in the mountains. Also, people walking and kids playing in the parks and streets, but between all those photos, there was one photo that was hanging on one of the walls alone; it was the most significant photo of a man in his early fifties, and on top of that photo, there was a countdown time and date.

Jacob sighed and read the time aloud, "16 hours until May 18th..."

"Thank you, Jacob, for reporting back on short notice." A voice interrupted Jacob's thoughts. It was coming from the end of the hall.

Jacob looked towards the source of the sound and, with a respectful smile, exclaimed, "Mr. President, it is always an honor to meet you."

The president came closer, and you could see his face. He looked like an early sixties man, dark skin, tall and lean with sharp eyes and a deep voice. His short, curly hair was a mix of salt and pepper. He smiled at Jacob and shook hands.

"Likewise, Jacob, we've been through a lot, my friend, and it's always a pleasure to work with you."

His tone changed to firm and serious as he continued, "But this time, it looks like things are getting out of control, and the council asked for an emergency meeting to deal with the sudden increase in traffic; they're looking for explanations and solutions, as time is ticking and one more incident on May 18th, may cause irreversible damage."

Jacob smiled while looking at the president. "Nothing is irreversible; we can fix it like before."

"What we did before was wrong; it was necessary then, but you saw what happened after that. We can't keep breaking our oath and pretending like nothing happened. We have to do the right thing using the right way; no more shortcuts! Besides, the council wouldn't allow that." The president's tone was firm.

Jacob nodded, agreeing with what the president said, and continued, "You know that I didn't approve of what happened in 1940, but we wouldn't be here if we hadn't taken action."

The president looked at him and said, "The council is here."

The room suddenly changed into a different shape; out of nowhere, there was a big, rounded table in the middle. The photos on the wall stayed as they were, but the dates and times filled the walls, the ceilings, and the floor, whereas the council members began to arrive one by one and gathered around the table. They all looked like statues with undefined, distorted shapes until the twelve members sat around the meeting table and looked at each other. Then, in a blink, they all changed their forms to look the same; they all looked just like Jacob!

Jacob smiled as he was looking at twelve duplicates of himself. That was always the council's method when integrating someone; they emulated the combined shape so they'd feel relaxed.

110

One of the council members asked Jacob to sit down as a chair appeared beside him.

Jacob sat down, and the president walked to the table and sat down to complete the circle of the thirteen council members, but he stayed in his shape with a warming smile on his face, unlike the other members. Their faces had no expression at all.

One of the council members looked at Jacob and said, "The traffic dropped to 50%, then increased to 150%. Do you have any explanation?"

Jacob sighed before crossing his finger in front of his face, looking straight into the council member's eyes as if he were looking at himself in a mirror. He said, "You know, whoever said ignorance is bliss was wrong; the real bliss and the real shelter is knowledge, and we were blessed by one of our crew, who has the knowledge that could save all of us."

All council members were silently listening to Jacob, including the President!

Jacob remembered a quotation from a Human book called 'The Complete Life's Little Instruction Book.'

"Be brave, even if you are not, pretend to be; no one can tell the difference."

He said to himself, "Looks like this quote works on Afreets as well; in the end, we are all the same."

Then, with the same confident smile, he looked at the Council members and told them what caused the traffic to slow down and then build up again to 150%. He said, "Before the deadline, the traffic will go down to less than 50%, but this time, we will be able to control it forever."

He said that while pointing to the countdown time on top of the big photo of that man, as the time was now starting to count down to 15 hours.

The council members started talking to each other while some started drawing graphs with the names of Laura, Terry, and David on its axis. In a firm voice, the President looked at Jacob and said, "Jacob, no matter what you do, whatever happened in 1940 won't happen again."

Jacob nodded, agreeing with the president's statement, "Yes, Mr. President, it won't happen again."

The Council members finished talking, and one of them looked at Jacob and said, "All the calculations point to Suzan replacing David. What if that didn't happen?"

Jacob replied, "It will happen, but even if it didn't happen, then we have no choice but to perform the control operation."

A council member said, "But the control operation will make us lose the privilege of knowledge and power. Besides, you can't launch it with that glitch in the system." He pointed to one of the photos on the corner of the front wall.

"Yes, but it will guarantee our survival; control operation is our last resort, and we would use it only if they failed the Quiz. And don't worry about the glitch; we will fix it tonight."

With that said, he stood up and started walking towards the door, passing the countdown time and reading the date next to it: May 18th, 1889.

As he left the room, he muttered, "It won't happen again."

The Inscription

"That's it, Nothing else!" John was wondering, looking at the translation of the inscription on Joseph's laptop, before he swallowed the last piece of the Kunafa.

Suzan crossed her fingers in front of her face and eyebrows, thinking deeply about the translation. Joseph was looking at the translation, and a subtle smile started to find its way on his lips before it became a big smile of victory.

"Don't you see it, Uncle John!!, this message says a lot." Joseph sounded exhilarated, exciting voice.

Suzan looked at Joseph. With a face full of question marks, "Did you get something we're missing here?"

John looked to Joseph for his answer. Joseph relaxed his back on his chair and pointed to the laptop, saying, "Let us read it again."

Without waiting for their answer, he started to read the translation aloud,

"My Queen, and the queen of all queens,

You are my wife and the purpose of my life,

You are the Shelter from disaster and the path to eternity.

You are the Beginning, and you are the End, but with you, every end is a new beginning,

Your eyes are the maze and the Exit, as they are the secret of all secrets."

Joseph finished reading and looked at his mom and uncle, awaiting their response.

Suzan and John looked at each other and then at Joseph before John broke the silence, asking Joseph, "What is new? We read it many times; how is that helping us to solve this riddle?"

Suzan followed, "Joseph, can you explain to us what you see in this message that we don't?"

Joseph sighed. Before he stood up and poured himself a big glass of milk, took a big sip, and relaxed on his seat, looked at them and said, "OK, Akhenaton wrote many love letters to his wife Nefertiti, on walls, on temples, and papyrus, but why would he write a love letter to her on that statue and in a secret code?"

Suzan and John started to pay more attention. "K, keep going."

Joseph smiled and took another sip, then continued, "There is one reason that made him write this letter to Nefertiti on that thing," he paused for a second, looking at them before continuing, "The only reason to explain this letter is that Nefertiti is that Statue!"

Both John and Suzan nodded their heads, not accepting this theory before. Suzan looked at Joseph, saying, "Joseph, I know you are excited to figure out this puzzle, but what you're saying is way too much and far to believe. Nefertiti is a well-known queen in Egyptian history; how come she is that statue? And even if we assumed someone made that statue and didn't finish it, why did they put the inscription on it? And why is there no mention of it anywhere in the history references? Besides, you saw this thing in the bathroom, and both of you saw it in the King's room in the museum, so are you telling me that what you saw was Nefertiti by herself and that she's still alive?!"

Suzan was expecting Joseph to retract what he said about his theory, which was nearly impossible, but surprisingly, Joseph was calm and looked at his mom and said, "Mom, since this journey started and everything we are facing is near to impossible, however, it is happening. To answer your questions, no, what we saw in the bathroom and the king's room was not Nefertiti; it was another thing, and yes, Nefertiti is still alive, or let's say, she still exists!"

Suzan looked at him and said, "OK, based on your theory that Nefertiti was or is this thing, even so, we still don't have any information that could help us with this inscription."

Before Joseph answered her, he looked at his uncle, who was looking at him, paying full attention. He smiled and asked, "What do you think, Uncle John?"

John's smile filled his face, and he said, "It took me a while to figure it out!" He looked at Suzan and said, "If this statue is for Nefertiti, then this inscription is saying a lot!"

Before Suzan could reply, Joseph explained his theory further: "OK, I want you to think about our conversation with Michael about the multidimensional universe, consider Adam's diary, and then listen carefully to Akhenaten's message to Nefertiti. Can you do that?"

They both nodded their heads, and Joseph smiled and continued, "he started by calling his wife the queen of all queens; we might think he exaggerated to praise his wife, but he meant that she's from a royal family, but we all know that she was not, at least from all the information we have about Nefertiti. And then he said that she's his wife and the purpose of his life. Akhenaten was like a philosopher, so even with a love message to summarize the purpose of his life in his wife, it is a little too much unless she is not just a wife but something more. Then he said she was the shelter from disaster and the path to eternity. You can only take shelter from disaster if you can forecast it, and the eternity is…" He paused and looked into their eyes before pressing his words, "TIME, and in our world, time is the fourth dimension. Remember our talk with Michael?"

Suzan's mouth was open; her eyes dazzled, and her face became tense; hearing her son analyzing the inscription that way, John's smile didn't leave his face.

Suzan seemed amazed. Joseph's face blushed from how his mother looked at him, and then he continued, "He followed that by saying she is the beginning and the end. Again, he talks about time, a new beginning with every end. Could you guys think about something that never ends, and its end is the beginning?"

"The infinity sign, or the lazy eight." They answered in chorus.

Joseph nodded and continued, "Yes, the two alphas meeting each other to make the sign, to represent the beginning and the end for us, but for them, every beginning is the end, and every end is a new beginning in a different universe...."

Suzan interrupted Joseph, "But who are they? Them."

John smiled and said, "The answer is in the last line; *your eyes are the maze and the exit, as they are the secret of all secrets.*"

Then he looked at Joseph and said, "But This means we need to get a 3D print of Nefertiti's face statue!"

Joseph smiled, walked to the printer, came back with a 3D print of Nefertiti's face, and looked at his uncle, saying, "When we were at the museum, I took a few photos of her statue right before we met Sarah."

John laughed out loud, hugging his nephew, and looked at Suzan, saying, "I wish I were as smart as him."

Suzan said, smiling, "You are, indeed!" Then she asked, "But how will this statue help us?"

"Her eyes are the secret of all secrets!"

Joseph continued, "Nefertiti's statue had perfect eyes with incredible symmetry, a symmetry that doesn't exist in real life, and that is the secret: it was sculptured like that for a reason; it is not just the eyes of a queen; it is a template that will break the code and tell us the secret of all secrets."

Suzan was trying to digest all this information before asking, "But where are we going to apply this template?"

John said, "We will start with the inscription itself; maybe there is another message hidden between the letters, then we will try the coffin."

Suzan nodded. "I have another question; if Nefertiti is still alive, and she was not the thing you saw in the bathroom, then who is she?"

"Sarah."

Suzan already knew the answer to that question, but she needed to hear it from John and Joseph, and yes, she listened to the answer as she expected, but it wasn't John or Joseph who spoke. It was Jacob who had been sitting at the table with them since the beginning.

Chaos

John jumped from his chair, trying to get a knife from the kitchen. At that exact moment, Suzan rushed to get Joseph away from Jacob. Joseph froze in his place with a face full of fear, but his worry turned into a frightening scream as he saw his mom and his uncle push back into their chairs right before that Thing showed up next to him and put its hand around his neck.

John, struggling through the pain all over his body, looked at the Thing, shouting, "Don't you dare hurt him!"

Suzan screamed, "Joseph!" She started sobbing while pleading, "Please, please, don't hurt my son, please."

Jacob kept calm and pointed towards the Thing, who slowly took his hands off Joseph's neck and stepped back.

Suzan spoke softly out of her tears, "Thank you."

Jacob looked into John's eyes, "Hello, John, I was looking forward to meeting you; Sarah spoke so well about you."

Then, he looked at Suzan. "How are you, Suzan? How is your research going so far on that nasty virus?"

"Who are you?" Joseph asked.

Jacob looked at Joseph with a smile and said, "Hello, Joseph. I am sorry I didn't introduce myself; you can call me Dr. Jacob. I believe Sarah mentioned my name to you when you visited the museum."

"Where is Sarah?" John asked.

Jacob smiled as he looked at John before he sighed and said, "The council decided to exile her from this mission, as she violated the rules for the second time."

John felt cross and confused. "Council…Exiled…Who are you, and what is this Thing?" he said, pointing to the Thing, but then, he put his hand down with a perplexed face as the Thing suddenly disappeared, just as it had appeared.

Jacob looked at the three of them and waited for more questions. Only then, Suzan asked, "How did you get in here?"

Jacob smiled, "The answer to this question depends on what you mean by the word… here.!"

Before waiting for her response, he continued, "Here could mean your house as what you see in this world but from another perspective or, let me say, in a different dimension. This place could mean a street, public park, or even a presidential palace."

He paused for a second so they could understand what he said, then continued, "But to be more specific, in my world, this place is the presidential Palace, and I just had a formal interview with the council at this specific room, and they were all sitting around that table." He paused and continued with a smile, "Not that specific table, but another table at the same spot."

"Are you from the future?" John asked in a slow, perplexed voice.

"No, He is not from the future; he is from another dimension." Joseph said in a low voice, looked full of admiration for Jacob, and continued in the same low voice, "Michael was right!"

Jacob smiled and looked at Joseph with the same admiration. "To be more specific, we are four-dimensional creatures, something your world would call supernatural demons. Also, sometimes, you confuse us with ghosts, but we are using the name Afreets." then he sighed and said in a sarcastic tone, grinding his teeth, "Yes, Michael was right."

He then turned to John and said, "For us, there is no future or past; what you count as time is just another dimension like heights in your world so that we can move in that dimension forward and backward, but with limitations."

He continued, "We have our own time, and that is the 5th dimension, and for you, that is what it is called," he paused again, then continued in a slow, firm voice, "The Multiverse."

Suzan looked at him angrily. "So, you are behind those nanobots we thought were a virus; why?"

Jacob nodded his head. "Yes, Suzan, we are the ones who created those nanobots, and if you want to know why, then you'll need to translate the coded message on Akhenaten's coffin."

Joseph interrupted him, "What did you mean when you said you can move forward and backward with limitations?"

John followed with another question, "And what did you mean by that Sarah was exiled because she violated the rules twice?"

Jacob smiled and looked at Suzan, "How about you? Do you have a question, too?"

Suzan looked straight into his eyes and said, "Did you kill David?"

Jacob looked at her, held her hands, and pressed them with compassion. "No, Suzan, it was not my decision to kill David, as it was not my decision to kill Terry and Laura, for that matter."

Joseph screamed and rushed and jumped from his chair to his mom and threw himself between her arms while Suzan gasped and John bellowed, "What…did you kill Terry and Laura?"

Jacob sounded sorry and apologetic. "All those killings were not under my watch; things were not supposed to move on that route. No one was supposed to be killed."

Suzan's eyes filled with tears and anger. "No one was supposed to be killed! How about all the people who were killed by your nanobots? Were they also not under your watch?"

"No, Suzan, those were selected by a high-tech program that decides who can survive and who cannot, and that is based on a future predicted program. During my entire service, I didn't kill or order to kill anyone," he paused for a second before he continued, "I didn't kill anyone except this one time, and that was to save all of you, all of us, to be more specific."

Then he looked at Joseph and said, "I am sorry that you lost your dad; it is not fair for a kid your age to lose his dad, but since when is life fair? You may not understand it now, but that was the best course of action based on all calculations."

He continued, "I know you have many questions and confused feelings, but everything will become clear after you translate the code. Nothing I'd say now will ease the situation, but after you read the Pharaoh's message, you will better understand all the facts."

He continued after the pause...

"My appearance looked like chaos with some facts to learn and more questions to ask, but think of it as an introduction to the Pharaoh's message. Without this visit, you would miss a lot of information."

He looked at Suzan, who was about to say something, and said, "Not now, Suzan. I will answer your questions, but not now."

Suzan seemed surprised as she was about to ask Jacob a question, but then she decided to listen and save her question for later.

Joseph wiped up his tears, sat on his chair, and entered some data into the computer program Fatima gave him. Suzan and John sat on their chairs. John looked towards Jacob and said, "Who was that only person you killed to save all of us?"

Jacob looked like he remembered things that happened years and years ago. He sighed, looked at John, and said, "Read the Pharaoh's message first, then everything will make sense and fall into place."

He paused for a second before saying, "Everything…"

The Beginning

"Dr. Jacob, we need you urgently at the space lab." A man in a uniform with a big sign of infinity on his chest said that as he walked into Jacob's office. He seemed excited.

Jacob looked at him with his calm facial expression and sharp eyes. "Slow down, son; why didn't you send a brain signal instead of coming all the way here?"

"I wanted to see your facial reaction when I delivered the news to you."

Jacob's face stayed still as he asked the soldier, "OK, what news?"

The soldier paused briefly before saying excitedly, "We solved the code, and we can read the message!"

Jacob crossed his eyebrows, asking, "Did you read it?"

The soldier looked frustrated as he was expecting a different reaction from Jacob, but then he put on his formal facial responses back and said, "No sir, we are waiting for you at the lab."

Jacob smiled and said, "OK, let us go and read this message."

They walked on this long hallway till they reached somewhere that looked like a space shuttle. They closed the door behind them, and the soldier pushed a few buttons before the door opened to a different hallway; they both walked into the room till the end; the soldier opened the door as Jacob walked in, followed by the soldier and then the door closed.

"I heard you solved the code. Are we sure this time?" Jacob asked a scientist in her white coat as she looked at a big monitor in front of her.

"Yes, Dad, this time we found the right code," Sarah said as she looked at the soldier, smiling, "You look lost; I told you; nothing so far could impress my dad."

The soldier nodded, saying, "Right, the same calm face no matter what!"

Jacob had a subtle smile on his face. He looked at Sarah, saying, "OK, where is the message?"

Sarah stood up and walked to a big wall across the room. She clicked a button on her watch, and the whole wall turned into a 3D screen. She pointed towards some holograms on that screen.

"As you know, we received signals from space that looked like a long-encrypted message, and all our engineers and scientists couldn't solve this code, and it took us three hundred rotations of our planet around the sun to solve the code, but today, we can proudly announce that we can read it!"

Jacob nodded, saying, "We knew this message came from space, as we believe there are different civilizations on other galaxies, and…"

Sarah interrupted him, "It was not from a different galaxy. I am sure there are multiple lives on other galaxies, and one day, we will communicate with them, but not this time. This message was not from another galaxy, it's from…"

Jacob interrupted her this time, "Did you read it?"

Sarah replied, "No, I was waiting for this moment to read it with you after all the hard work we've been through to solve this puzzle. However, we wouldn't be able to read this message."

She continued with a smile as she saw wonder on her father's face. "We will Watch the message; it was an encrypted video signal."

Jacob was listening carefully before asking, "You said this message was not from space, so where is it from?"

Sarah pressed her words slowly, saying, "This message was from a different Universe!"

Jacob crossed his eyebrows and leaned forward on his chair while crossing his hands in front of his face, repeating what his daughter had said, "From a different Universe?!"

Sarah took a deep breath before continuing, "Yes, Dad, this message was from another Universe, and the one who sent it didn't send it just to us, but to the multiverse!"

Jacob's eyebrows crossed more before saying, "Multiverse! So, is it real? And how did you know it is from a different universe and that it was sent as a global message?"

Sarah turned to the big screen and pressed a few buttons on her watch. As the screen changed to show codes and algorithms, she explained, "All our assumptions were based on the fact that this message came from a different civilization on the galaxy or another galaxy, and all these assumptions failed to decode the message. We were about to give up until I met Hagar from the Biophysics lab, and she told me about her research." She said that as she pointed to a young woman sitting at the end of the lab.

Hagar walked to the front of the lab, standing next to Sarah before she pointed to another hologram and looked at Jacob, saying, "As we know, we are living in a four-dimensional world; the theory we were studying at my lab is, what if there is a three-dimensional world that lives amongst us and…"

She stopped talking as everyone in the room started giggling and laughing about her theory; everyone except Dr. Jacob who looked around at everyone in the room with his firm eyes, and as he looked, everyone became silent. He looked back at Hagar and nodded his head as a sign to continue; Sarah smiled and looked at Hagar. Hagar nodded thankfully before explaining her theory, "What if this world of three dimensions is amongst us? What if there are two dimensions and one-dimensional worlds as well? What if there is a five-dimensional world? We'd be sure these worlds can share the same space, but they can't see or fill each other unless we find the right energy level to break these barriers between them." She paused for a second and took a deep breath.

She went on, "I focused on the three-dimensional world and started to design a simulated computer program on how this world will look like and how we could interact with this world. I also tried to figure out what language they would use and how they would communicate. It took me many trials until I found an algorithm to simulate this world."

Sarah continued, "This is when I got the idea; what if this message was from that three-dimensional world? But if that were the case, we would feel a disturbance in our planet's energy level when the message arrives, which didn't happen. That left us with one option: this message was from a three-dimensional world but in another universe. So, I used the algorithm that Hagar designed to decode the message, and the results came…as…" She pointed to the hologram before proudly declaring, "a 100% match!"

Jacob's face was calm until both Sarah and Hagar finished. He looked at them with pride and said, "If this is true, it means that we could communicate with the fifth dimension…"

He paused and said, "TIME".

Everyone in the lab was stunned, and someone started clapping for Sarah and Hagar. Everyone in the lab followed and started cheering for them.

Dr. Jacob had a calm smile. He looked at Sarah and said, "Now, let us watch the message."

They all sat down as Sarah started to push some buttons on her watch, and a hologram began to shape in the middle of the lab.

Everyone in the lab froze from the surprise; that was the first time Dr. Jacob's face lost its peace. He turned pale; in the middle of the room was a hologram of Dr. Jacob himself!

"Hello, Sarah; I never doubted that you would figure out the code of this message. In the end, this is what you did here at the beginning, and I never thought we would reach this phase, as we are admitting our failure and trying to save ourselves. But on another universe, it looks like it is inevitable fate; that no matter what we do, the end is coming in 2025 on the three-dimensional earth."

The message kept going. Sarah looked at her father and realized that there was finally something that could impress her dad, as Jacob was not just impressed, he was …scared!

Dr. Jacob's hologram said, "Now I need to talk to myself, so clear the room. Everyone looked at Dr. Jacob, who nodded, and they all left the room except Sarah!

The Hologram of Dr. Jacob smiled and said, "Everyone, including you, Sarah." Sarah paused out of surprise and said, "Can you…"

The Hologram interrupted her and said, "No, Sarah, I cannot see you, but this is exactly what happened here many years ago; now, can I talk to myself alone?"

Sarah started to walk out of the lab when the Hologram called her, "Sarah."

She turned to see the hologram of her dad looking at her with eyes full of love. He said, "I love you too!"

Sarah looked confused as she had never seen this look in her dad's eyes, and she'd never seen him that emotional. For a second, she wished the hologram was her real Dad so she could just throw herself in his arms and tell him she loved him too. She paused for a second and then left the room!

The Hologram looked at Dr. Jacob and breathed deeply as his face calmed down. With sharp eyes and a deep voice, he said, "Now listen to me, Jacob, and mark my words carefully."

This time, Jacob wasn't just scared; he was frightened!

The Conference

Dr. Jacob was standing on the stage next to Sarah and Hagar, and two more scientists were chatting and discussing scientific terms. Many people entered the conference room and took their seats before the room was filled with an audience. The room's walls were covered with framed photos of different scenes, and all photos were three-dimensional: of parks, oceans, and streets. The audience was astonished at those photos; they looked different and weird.

Dr. Jacob started talking calmly, with his sharp eyes looking at the audience.

"There is no easy way to say what I am about to tell you. So, I need your full attention, as what we are about to tell you is not just one discovery but multiple discoveries in many fields that will change how we look at life forever. What you're about to witness today could be the reason for our survival or extinction."

The audience started to get worried, and side talk began to rise; only then did a strong voice come out, "We are all ears, Dr. Jacob. Please proceed." A mixed reaction came from the audience. Some of them were anxious.

Jacob smiled, "Thank you, Mr. President."

Then he took a deep breath and started talking, "Since one hundred planet rotations around our sun, we could read an encrypted message received four hundred years ago…"

One of the audience interrupted him, asking, "YEARS!! What does that mean?"

Dr. Jacob ignored the question and continued.

"This message was not from the space or another Galaxy. This message was from me in another universe where I was in the three-dimensional world." He looked at the person who asked the question and continued, "In this world, they use the term YEAR for one rotation of the planet around the sun."

He paused briefly, looking at the audience to see how far they understood his words. Then he continued, "There are many universes, not just one, but almost infinity, with every choice we make, with every decision we take; a new universe is created, and this message was the first communication among this multiverse, but because of the space-time, these universes are functioning on a different period. The message we received was from a universe in the year 2025 AD, which is for us, in the future, based on our calculations and our studies of the other universe's civilizations. Our universe is in the year one million BC; this message was from the future, almost one million years from now."

This time, the president asked, "Dr. Jacob, what is in this message?"

Hagar told the president, "The message says that the world will end in 2025 AD because of the three-dimensional creatures known as Humans."

Sarah continued… "As you see in those photos, these are the humans (creatures) in different universes. For years, we have been trying to discover the gate between our world and their world, and finally, with the help of the message we received, we were able to discover the gate that would allow us to enter their world. We could also study their past and future after successfully communicating with the multiverse on the three-dimensional level. We are still working on communicating with our four-dimensional peers, but until we succeed in that, saving the world from Armageddon is our responsibility."

Someone from the audience interrupted Sarah and asked, "I'm trying to follow what you are saying, so, in our universe, the world will end after one million years in the three-dimensional world; how long is that in our world?"

"Six months," one of the scientists replied. He looked like a robot with a face and voice lacking feeling.

"For this three-dimensional world, the fourth dimension is time; as for us, the fifth dimension is also time. Moving on to the fourth dimension in our universe is a challenge. We can only jump for a few days or dive for a few days, but we can't make big leaps to see their future. The same is the case with height dimensions. They can only jump slightly higher or dive a little lower, but soon, they can move with speed almost as fast as the speed of light on that dimension. We knew that studying their world on different universes would help us start predicting our future. The process was very sophisticated and dynamic as on every second."

He paused for breath. "A second is another unit to measure the small amounts of time in their world."

"Every second, several universes are born, and many others collapse. But it was all under control with a slow predicted slope until we found the pattern always getting disturbed, and the slope changed dramatically around 1889, specifically on May 18th of that year. Then, a big disturbance was experienced in the 1920s before the universe vanished in 2025. All our studies show those dates as 100% accurate, and the question was, *what could we do to save our universe from this fate?!*"

The president was concerned, "What happened in the 1920s that caused this disturbance?"

"We don't know yet." Jacob answered briefly, then continued, "That is why we decided to interfere and study this world closely."

"Is it possible?" multiple audiences asked, wondering.

Dr. Jacob replied, "I am here today to seek permission from the president and the council to send volunteers to the human world to study it and reach an agreement to save our universe from that fate."

The audience started to discuss and have side talks, and then the president looked at Jacob and said, "You have permission, Dr. Jacob, and I need a daily meeting conference with you. Choose your team and keep me updated with all the details."

Dr. Jacob smiled and looked at his team. He then looked at the president and nodded with a confident, respectful smile. "Thank you, Mr. President; a week from now will be our day of victory. Victory Day"

The president asked, "So which of these photos is our three-dimensional world universe?"

Dr. Jacob smiled and said, "None, all of these photos are from different universes. This is our three-dimensional universe," he said and pressed a button.

In the middle of the room was a hologram of three buildings in the center of a big city, on the side of a beautiful river. he smiled and said, "In the Human's language, they call these buildings…Pyramids."

Nefertiti

"The Pyramids!! How?" Akhenaten wondered, asking Nefertiti, then he continued, "You said the earth was on one million years BC, and now we are on 1350 BC, and thanks for explaining to me what is BC, and why the years are counted down, then counted up, but the pyramids were not that old, it could be a thousand or two thousand years old, but not a one million years! If we'd built the pyramids that long ago, then we should now be…"

He paused as Nefertiti smiled and said, "Looks like you figured out what I was going to say."

Akhenaten was still surprised by what he thought he was about to discover, then said, "I want to hear it from you; what did your people do to my people?"

Nefertiti looked at his eyes and said, "We saved your civilization, and I will tell you how."

She tried to calm him down before she continued to explain what had happened to him. She asked, "But first, tell me why you named me Nefertiti?"

He smiled and looked at her with love. "Nefertiti means; *A Beautiful Woman Has Come*, and that is you, my queen, a beautiful woman, who has come to steal my heart and be my soul."

Sarah giggled and said, "The first time you saw me, you called me Afreet."

Akhenaten laughed, "The first time I saw you, I was scared to death. I was walking at the palace, and you were sneaking on me, but you stayed on the phase between the two worlds; only then did you disappear to appear again, as you are now, my Queen and the Queen of all queens."

With that, he leaned forward and kissed her lips softly, a kiss that made her face blush, and in a breaking voice, she said, "No matter how many times you kiss me, every time feels like the first time."

He smiled and said, "You broke the orders and decided to stay here with me; why?"

She acted angry, then laughed and said, "How many times do I need to tell you?"

He looked at her and said, "No matter how many times you say it, every time feels like the first time."

She smiled and looked at his eyes, then held his hands and said, "Because I loved you at first sight, I couldn't see you as the pharaoh of the modern world. I saw you as a man, husband, and father of my children."

He held her hands, looked into her eyes, and said, "It is meant to be."

She gazed at nowhere before saying in a low voice, "No, it is not."

"What do you mean?"

"I mean you and me together, as husband and wife, never happened in any other universe. What we are doing here is changing the whole equation, which will lead to other consequences."

He looked at her and asked, "Are you saying we will never get married on all multiverses?"

She replied, "Yes, at least on all the universes we studied so far."

He smiled at her and said, "Love changes everything. Maybe Akhenaten was not that handsome in other universes."

They laughed, and then, he asked her, "Now, tell me, how come the pyramids were built more than a million years ago?"

She sighed and said, "I'll tell you what the deal with the ancestors was."

The Ancestors

Place: Dr. Jacob's office

Date: Unknown

Time: Does not exist

Dr. Jacob was checking some documents on his desk and started drawing three-dimensional shapes of pyramids and cubes. Then he sent a brain signal to one of the scientists, and in no time, the door was opened, and the scientist walked into the office. Dr. Jacob gestured for him to sit down!

Dr. Jacob asked, "Why didn't you attend the meeting? They asked for you."

"They wanted to ask about our experiments on those primitive creatures who call themselves Humans and our progress on time travel. I couldn't attend the meeting as I was busy with some lab results."

Dr. Jacob did not buy that, but he decided to let it go for now; at the same time, he sent a brain signal to Sarah and Hagar, and they were knocking on the door in almost no time. They sat in front of Jacob, who looked at the three of them and said...

"As you know, we succeeded in establishing a communication line with other universes on the four-dimensional level, so finally, we were able to talk to the same kind of civilization as ours, but unfortunately, every Universe was moving on a different time span and that creates differences not just on human level, but on our level as well. The good news is, we reached an agreement on how to save all of us, and it will be our task, as we are the youngest universe among the multiverses."

He paused to make sure they were following him before he continued.

"Human races have a lot of potential to rule the multiverse. They even have the potential to communicate with other civilizations around the globe and to communicate with other universes, and in one of those universes, they had theories about the speed of light, and more than that, about the superstring theory, but…"

He paused as he was about to deliver the bad news that usually follows that word!

Hagar felt so excited, "Dr. Jacob, this is great news, and we can work with them to ensure we're all safe. Ultimately, we might misinterpret the message that humans are our savior, not our executioner!"

The scientist looked at her cynically in a sarcastic way and said, "It is good to be that optimistic, but I don't think we will see anything good from these creatures."

Sarah was looking and following what her dad said as Dr. Jacob looked at them and continued talking. And they did not interrupt him.

"As I was saying, they have all the potential to succeed but also all the greed and arrogance, arrogant to destroy what they built; if we let them drive, they will destroy themselves and everyone else."

He sighed and started to look at the three-dimensional shape and said, "For now, as I mentioned, they are at one million BC, and they already built Pyramids in an area called Egypt. These Pyramids are designed to be power generators and laser guns; imagine what they could achieve in a hundred thousand years!"

This time, Sarah interrupted him and asked, "You said it would be our task as we are the youngest universe in spacetime, but how long do we have until the rest of the universes reach 2025? Some of them had already reached it, and they vanished."

Dr. Jacob looked confused and said, "I wish I had a clear answer to that, but from what I know from the meeting, is that we have the time until our universe hits that date, so it is one million years on Earth or six months on our world."

"What did other Universes do to control humans, and did it work?" Hagar asked.

The scientist replied, "They all started late, so whatever they are doing will not have the same effect, but this is not the case with us; we have the time. He laughed sarcastically and continued, "We have the time."

Dr. Jacob looked at the three of them and said, "The human race needs to live in a maximum 5,000-year period, then we will reevaluate every period to see if we need to reduce or increase it."

Sarah looked surprised. "We are wiping out their memories, but that is unfair!"

The scientist replied, "Not wiping out their memories, but we will make them slightly lose the time track, then forget the major events, as we need for them to work and do their research, but within until certain limits; believe me, even that is not enough."

Hagar looked at him. "Not enough; what else do you want to do to them?"

Dr. Jacob replied in one word, "Virus!"

Sarah and Hagar were confused, while the scientist smiled, proudly saying, "My graduation project..." he paused, and then continued, "...in a different universe."

Dr. Jacob had a subtle smile on his face as he looked at Sarah and Hagar and continued, "From what we studied on other universes, humans love to fight, creating troubles and making enemies, and then fight with each other, or fighting nature and destroying earth, so we need to redirect these fights. We need to redirect their research. Therefore, instead of inventing killing machines, they will invent medicines; instead of killing each other, they will meditate and be quarantined. Because of this virus, one of their greatest scientists, Isaac Newton, invented calculus and changed the human world. He could find the laws of physics and define gravity just by observing an apple falling from a tree during his quarantine. Believe me, we are doing them and us a favor."

Sarah disagreed and still refused the idea. "But this is not fair; you gave them selective memory, then you make them sick; what else are you going to do with them?"

Dr. Jacob replied, "We will scare them, make them think about supernatural powers, demons and angels, witches and wizards, we will make them scared to keep them under control."

Hagar looked at him and said, "Then what? Why do we need to do all of that? Why don't we wipe off all this race?"

This time, Sarah replied to Hagar as she looked into her dad's eyes. "Because we need them, we need to study this race in our universe; we can't rescue wiping them off before making sure that this extermination will not affect our race, right, Dad?"

She said that in a challenging tone, full of anger.

Dr. Jacob sighed and said, "No, Sarah, not just because of what you said. I want to give this race a chance, but I can't rescue our race and everyone's life by letting this race thrive. Consider it a quiz; we will see if they can pass it. As we said, we will reevaluate every 5,000 years and decide on the next phase. I need the three of you to be on the field, so please delegate all your projects at the lab to your peers and prepare for the trips to Earth."

Then he pointed to the scientist and said, "You and I will work together."

He pointed towards Hagar and said, "You will go first, then Sarah after you. How you enter this world will make you look scary, and your shapes will be undefined, but then you can transform into a familiar shape in that three-dimensional world. These trips will consume a lot of energy and disturb our systems' energy, so we must use them wisely. You can be anywhere and everywhere, with no limits, but don't interfere with their actions, as we don't want to be the reason to create more universes. If it happens and you interfere, you must report immediately so we can make our calculations and fix the timespan. Hence, even if your actions create another universe, we will ensure it's wiped out. Any questions?"

The scientist looked at Jacob and asked, "We still don't know the reason that will cause the end of our universe?"

Dr. Jacob paused briefly, then said, "That is why we need to be in the field and watch them closely."

Hagar asked, "I still can't get it; how could one person cause the end of the universe?"

Dr. Jacob crossed his eyebrows and said softly and in a low voice, "It needs only one person who knows what he's doing to build a whole universe or destroy another." Then he continued louder, "We still don't know if it was one person or a group. Anyway, what we are doing here was never done in any other universe before, so we will start what we agreed on, and who knows, maybe the fate will change in our universe."

But he was wrong; fate never changes. It may come sooner or later and in different forms, but in the end, it will be at your doorstep and get in without even knocking, and for sure, it did!

Fate

Akhenaten listened to Nefertiti until she finished talking and kept looking at her. "I know it is hard to assimilate all these facts, but that was the best course of action at this time, and…"

He interrupted her, looking straight into her eyes. He said, "Facts!!! What facts? I don't know now what is real and what is fiction; you stole our history; do you have any idea what our human race could achieve if we had all this knowledge?"

She smiled and said, "Yes, my dear, I have an idea what your human race could achieve if we didn't interfere; I don't just have an idea; I saw it with my own eyes. I saw the damage, the destruction, the war, and the killing, and I saw your human race's extinction and the earth vanishing. I saw that on different universes, not just once or twice, but every time, and even the universe that tried to keep you distracted with diseases and failed to keep you under control. You ended up with the same fate: we couldn't rescue the same scenario in our world."

He looked at her in frustration and said, "So why didn't you simply wipe out all of us or control us like slaves? Oh wait…you are already controlling us like slaves!"

She tried to stay calm, as she sensed the anger in his voice, "We didn't wipe out all of you because we wanted to give your race a chance, and we didn't control you as slaves because your civilization and your existence were based on the ability to choose your decisions and then face the consequences, in all courses of history. All Your civilizations were based on trial and error, and by the way, on the other hand, your race is the one that started slavery and ranked people based on their color, religion, or nationality. Some of your race will claim they are different Blood and justify committing horrible crimes against another race. That victim race, after a while, will claim they are the chosen race and commit the same genocide against kids and women, and keeping the vicious cycle of destruction, your race, for ages and centuries, will discriminate against women, claiming superiority for men. You might not be aware of these things now, but it's happened in different universes, and it will keep happening here."

She felt an anger in her voice. She took a deep breath, looked at him straight in the eyes, held his hand in a calm voice, and said, "But you know what else I saw in your human race's history? I saw civilization, sacrifices and love, science and art, activists and rebels facing dictators, feminists, and liberals, but most importantly, I saw diversity."

"Diversity?!" he asked, wondering.

She smiled as she sensed his voice returning to reasoning and calm, "Yes, my king, diversity; I saw eras of accepting others, no matter the differences. I saw your race, seeing the difference between accepting and agreeing. Yes, there will be dark eras of hate and wars, but I saw your race overcome these dark ages and jump over them to accept and live together in peace, but again, we couldn't risk leaving you in full control."

"The Universe that left us uncontrolled, how long did they last?" he asked.

She looked sad as she said, "Less than a one thousand years before they destroyed everything, including all higher dimensional creatures, we had to introduce to you other parameters like the virus to help you to survive, and so far, your race survived one million years."

He gave her a sarcastic laugh and said, "Yes, one million years, but every five thousand years, we turn to be like cavemen, as primitive creatures."

She smiled and said, "A primitive human with a chance to live is better than a dead astronaut."

"Astronaut? What's that?" he asked curiously.

She smiled, "I am breaking many rules here by telling you all this information, but it is a Greek word. Astron means a *star*, and nauts means *sailor*; your race will go to space, and the people who will go will be called *Astronauts*."

Akhenaten looked surprised; he said, "The Space! I always dreamed about that. Tell me, who was the first to enter the space?"

She laughed and said, "The first living creature that went to space was a dog called Laika!"

"A dog?!!!" he screamed out of surprise and then cracked laughing, trying to process all this information. Then he nodded and asked her, "OK, how did this virus help us to survive?"

"It unified your race for a while; it woke up your race to understand priorities; it reminded you that death is not that far and that it is not worth it to keep fighting over a short-term life; it helped your race to focus more on medical researches and medical formulas before you get back to your natural habit of being shortsighted and fight over mortal life, only then we sent you another quiz, sometimes you failed, and most of the times you passed."

"We already knew about mortal life, and we already knew that death is not that far; we embraced it and celebrated it and …"

She smiled and interrupted him, "And soon, you will forget about all these cultures and beliefs; you may be doing the right thing now, but you will shift until your race turns 180 degrees. Even with the virus, you will quarantine and start seeing life's real meaning. And some of you will keep these high morals, but then, you will shift back and accuse and blame each other. This is not our fault; this is how your race was designed, and that is why you need a wake-up call every once in a while."

"A wake-up call?"

She smiled. "Yes, that is a term your race will use in the future; it means a reminder or a shock to realize where you are positioned, where you're standing, and where you're going."

He looked at her, shaking his head as he started to understand her point, and then asked, "So there is no paranormal magic, no demons or wizards?"

She laughed and said, "Besides us, no. I don't think there are any of those, except if they are on different dimensions that we both can't see or sense."

He nodded. "I'm sure there are. In the end, you are only one level above, and from what you told me about this superstring theory, there are ten levels or more, but I think there are more. If the Universe is a multistory building, it is not just ten or twenty stories; it will be bigger than pyramids, it will be…" he paused, trying to find the right words.

She smiled and said, "Skyscrapers!"

He looked at her in confusion, so she explained, "Skyscraper is a term your race will use in the future in English, and it means a very tall building that looks like it's touching the sky."

He liked the expression. "Yes, a Skyscraper."

"Yes, you're right. In the end, we know just a bit little, but this little is far enough to keep this universe surviving for more than one million years, as long as it will take." Sarah continued

"So, you were talking about diversity and how that helped us to survive the dark times, but you also mentioned religions. What is that?"

She looked at him, trying to choose her words to simplify things for him, but simultaneously, she was astonished at how he could grasp all this information at once! "In the future, people will have different beliefs; they will all follow one God, but they will call this God by different names and worship God in different ways, which will be called religions. It will help your race with meditation, brainstorming, and seeing things from different perspectives. As I told you about diversity, but also, it will cause war and damage and, in many eras, it will cause genocide."

Her voice turned sad, and he could notice tears in her eyes. "We saw children killed, women raped, and civilizations destroyed because of different beliefs and religions."

"So, are religions bad?"

"No, Religions are not bad, but not accepting others' beliefs and the narrow look created by people who will claim they knew religions better than others, and they started to control people and condemn them if they didn't follow their orders; that is what is bad, not the religion itself."

He smiled and said, "But this is already happening now. The priests of Amon temple are controlling everything; they call me God, but they are the ones who have all the power."

"Maybe one day, that will change." She said with a sly smile on her face.

He looked at her, wondering, "What do you mean?"

"OK, this might be hard to understand, but so far, you are doing great on processing all this information. I can't tell you what to do or what not to do, as this will change the course of action; it must be your own decision based on your thinking and free will."

In a sarcastic tone, he said, "Free will? Do you even hear yourself?"

This time, she sounded upset. "Yes, Akhenaten, free will. Stop playing the victim here because you guys are not victims; your brains are designed to forget. If I asked you about things that happened last year, you would probably remember only half of the truth because of your human race's curse…"

He interrupted her. "Curse? Now we have a curse?!"

"Yes, you do; your curse is Ego; your race refuses to admit any weakness, always trying to cover it instead of accepting it and dealing with it. So, when you forget things, your brain starts to create events to fill the gap, and the only thing we did is fill the existing gaps."

"By giving us false memories?"

"No, by giving you true memories, but from another universe, something in the future that will be called The Mandela Effect."

"Mandela…what?"

"Don't worry about the terms, but simply, when people start to remember things that are different from reality when people see something, and they feel it happened before, it is because it simply happened before, but in a different universe, something that will be known as …deja vu."

She felt it was too much, so she put her hand on his hand and said, "We only use these two effects to fill the gap with the memories. We thought it would help you survive, and it worked, my king, for almost one million years in Earth time; it was working."

"Then what?"

"I don't know, the clock is ticking, and 2025 will be here, and we don't even know what is causing the Armageddon. Your civilization should be reset again within a few years so that we can keep the universe in survival mode till 2025."

Akhenaten paused momentarily and then said, "Something is weird. Time for you is just another dimension, and you can move back and forth, so why don't you go to the future, figure it out, and fix it?"

"We can't do that; we can't move back and forth at your time. This will require energy that will disturb your world's energy levels. Also, that will change the course of action, which means every time we look, the future will change, and it is the same with the past; that is why we can't interact."

She paused briefly and said, "We didn't know how to move forward and backward on the fourth dimension. Think of it as flying in space or diving in oceans, but then we could move forward and backward. We tried that once and compared it to another universe. We caused an irreversible event in your future."

She paused before saying in a very sorry voice, "Something your world will call World War I."

He repeated what she said in a low voice, "World War One!"

"Yes, and because of that, we condemned time travel in your world, then we decided just to look, but because just looking means changing the course of action due to the amount of energy emitted from our world into your world, we unintentionally caused another damage, something your world will know as World War II."

He sounded sarcastic as he didn't realize the damage those two wars had caused and said, "What caused World War 3?"

She looked at him and said in a scared voice, "If it had happened, that would be the end; as a matter of fact, we think that could be the reason for the end."

She continued, "That is why we can only predict based on what we are seeing in other universes and the current events happening in this one, then we can use our equations to find solutions, same as when you draw a three-dimensional shape on a paper to solve a geometrical problem, but none of these observations are telling us about how the end will come, we only know that the slope will get steeper, and things will accelerate starting in the 1920s, but we can't tell how and why!"

Akhenaten looked at her with a subtle smile before saying in an optimistic tone, "I think I can help you."

The Deal

"How?" Joseph stopped reading and looked at Jacob.

Suzan and John were sitting and listening to Joseph, who was reading the translation on the coffin after he applied the algorithm that took Nefertiti's eyes and applied it to the writings on the sarcophagus.

They both were amazed at how heliographic writing, which looked like ancient Egyptian stories for decades, became a story of the human race's biggest secret. They both looked at Jacob, waiting for an answer.

Jacob looked at the three of them with the same calm face and said, "What do you mean by how?"

Joseph looked surprised, "How did Akhenaten help you?"

"Why don't you finish reading so you will know," Jacob replied.

Joseph was now getting annoyed, "I am sure you know very well that when the inscription is done, it ends with Akhenaten saying he can help, nothing else."

Akhenaten was wise not to continue the story about the coffin, but you hadn't finished reading yet; there was another part on the casket, remember?"

Joseph nodded as he remembered the part of the coffin that looked different and had a sign of repetitive order, so he started to apply the new algorithm with the equation of Nefertiti's eyes' dimensions and waited. He expected the algorithm to return with all scenarios to read the inscription and narrow it down to one reading, but the computer came with only one reading with a few words. Joseph looked at the words and was astonished.

Suzan looked at her son and asked, "What is wrong, Joseph? What did the computer say?"

Without looking at her, Joseph slowly read what was written on the screen, "The deal, Dr. Jacob: free will."

Jacob looked at Joseph and said, "Yes, Joseph, the rest of the story is with me, but only you can decide the end."

Everyone looked confused as Jacob paused for a second, then explained what happened, "Moving from our dimensions to your world dimension was already causing energy disturbance that unfortunately caused a sequence of events; the time travel or just monitoring caused both World War 1 and World War 2. We noticed the disturbance happening in other universes, and we knew something wrong had happened, and because of that, we decided never to try time travel or look into the future of your world. We even set a law that considers this act as a crime of genocide— punishable by death."

Suzan looked at him and said, "Punishable by death? I thought you are immortals."

Jacob looked at her and smiled, "A mosquito with a 7-day lifespan would have a look at you and think you are immortal."

They all looked upset. John said, "So, you look at us as if we are just mosquitos?"

Jacob smiled and said, "That was just a metaphor. What I meant was everything is relative, and at the end, every creature has to meet his end—everything in this system will end up dying."

Suzan nodded, understanding as he continued, "No one is immortal."

Then he looked back at Joseph and said, "As I was saying, we couldn't travel in time or even watch or observe; did you ever hear about the double slit experiment?"

"No, what is this experiment?"

Suzan looked at Joseph and tried to explain to him, "I think Jacob wants to clear the idea why observing could cause disturbance in the timestream and create events that were not supposed to happen if we didn't look."

"It is something about quantum physics, simply to study if electrons and light are considered waves or particles, so if you bring a board with double slits and put a solid board behind it, then shoot bundle of electrons using electron guns, you will see wave patterns on the other side of the solid board, but if you put a device like a camera to monitor this bundle of light to watch the electrons and see how these electrons go through the slit, you will see a pattern of two slits on the solid board, as if the electrons changed their behavior from waves to particles when we started to watch it."

Joseph looked confused as John looked at them and said, "How do you expect him to understand what you're talking about? You confused me; what does this have to do with observing time?"

He stopped as he figured it out, "So when you were not observing, the timestream was acting like waves creating multi universes that will cancel each other eventually and leave us with one option, but when you monitored, we got two solid options, which means two different universes."

Jacob nodded and continued, "Yes, only two options, war or no war, but the human race will always go to the war option, and that is what happened, but then those two options, as a rule, kept creating more and more options, and eventually, this infinite space-time started to get crowded with universes, producing what we called later; Space-time Traffic Jam or STJ."

"I still don't understand what Akhenaten has to do with all of this?" John asked.

Jacob looked at Joseph and said, "What if we monitored this electron without creating any disturbance in energy that will change its behavior? What if, in this double-slit experiment, we shoot an electron, and then we shoot another camera at the same speed that acts exactly and looks exactly like that electron? Then, we just sit and watch how this electron will behave."

Joseph started understanding what happened and said, "And this camera was…"

John continued, "Akhenaten."

Jacob nodded his head, agreeing. "Yes, Akhenaten was the first human being to travel in time and probably the last."

He continued, "But to be able to do that, we had to make a deal that includes wins and sacrifices."

They all looked at him, waiting for the second part of the story.

Time

Nefertiti was looking at Akhenaten and still couldn't believe what she had just heard from him.

"You are crazy. Do you have any idea what you are asking for?"

He smiled and said, "Yes, my queen, I am asking for a chance to save humanity, a small sacrifice to save our history and hopefully our future."

She looked at him with a look of love and admiration that she couldn't hide and said, "But there is no guarantee that you will be successful. Besides, it's too risky as it could cost you your life."

"If I failed to save the future, then at least I would've saved history, and at least the day when we are all gone, we will be standing on a solid ground of knowledge and cultures. My life is a meager price for this cause, but if I succeed, I will achieve the dream of all humanity—Immortality!" His eyes sparkled as he spoke.

"Are you doing this for humanity or yourself?"

He smiled and looked at her, "O' my Queen, all these thousands of years on Earth, and you still didn't understand the nature of humans; there was never and will never be a pure cause without personal interest. Yes, people will keep doing the right thing, but there will always be this spark of personal glory—the glory of recognition for being a hero or the glory of heaven in the afterlife. The key is not to let this personal glory change how you do the right thing; you always need to do the right thing in the right way."

"And immortality is your glory?"

"With immortality comes knowledge, and with knowledge comes power."

He paused, then continued, "But with immortality also comes enough time to observe, and with observation comes experience and more knowledge to realize that no matter how long you stay, there will always be this moment when you will go, and what matters at this moment is not how long you lived, but what you did; and how you spent your time on earth."

"Are you a Pharaoh, a philosopher, God, or a scientist?!" she said skeptically. She looked at him with eyes full of admiration on how he could simplify his concept and convince her.

He smiled and said, "I am the solution to your dilemma and the key to finding the truth, but to do that, I first need to be a rebel."

She looked confused, so he smiled and stood up. He walked around her before he started explaining his idea, "If we unified together and shared our knowledge, we will be able to conquer time; you need a time spy, someone who knows what is happening and reports back to you, but at the same time, without creating any disturbance in the energy level of time-space that could lead to different events, so what you need is—an insider."

He stopped talking to give her a chance to understand his theory.

Nefertiti nodded and said, "OK, and you are that insider, but how?"

Akhenaten smiled and said, "This is where the part of being a rebel comes. "We can't share this plan with the priests, and we can't do that here at the palace, but when you were explaining to me what happened in the future on other universes, you talked about the power of religions, and I agree with you, especially here in Egypt; and this is exactly the tool that I will use."

"You will use religion as a tool...?!"

"I will use a new religion as a tool; I will change my name from Amenhotep IV to Akhenaten; this is the name you have been addressing me with; it is catchy, and I will reject God Amun and follow a new God named Aten represented by the Sun; and by this, I will be able to seize the priests' power and keep all the powers to myself."

"OK, this is exactly what happened on different universes in other eras. History repeats itself, but how will that help your plan to be an insider in the time-space?"

He smiled, "Be patient, my Queen."

Then, he continued talking about his idea, "With the new God and a new religion comes a new capital. Thebes will no longer be the capital; I will choose a new city on the far side and call it 'Akhenaton.' I will change the style of temples and the style of writings and drawings, and I will create…"

Nefertiti interrupted him, "Chaos!"

"No, I am creating a distraction. With everyone getting confused about the changes in politics and religion, we will have the time to work on our experiments at the new palace far away."

Nefertiti nodded and continued listening to Akhenaten's time travel theory.

"My scientists, whom I trust, will work with your scientists, but they should never know anything about their identity; this deal is just between me representing the human race and your people. Your part of the deal is to leave our history, no more memory control. You leave us to try and decide, and at the same time, I will be your eyes to tell you what caused the changes in the 20th century that led to the end of 2025. You can keep your other tools like the virus and Mandela effect, or déjà vu, but let our brain decide how to use it and let our race decide how to fight their battles. Your part of this deal is to give us 'free will' and let us decide our future based on our history. The other part is to give me the freedom to move from body to body."

The Experiment

Jacob stopped talking and looked at the three of them to ensure they were following. Suzan looked at him and asked, "The freedom to move from body to body, what does that mean?"

Jacob looked at her and said, "Even with an insider, you are still disturbing the energy level of time, and we can't risk that, so the experiment was not time travel. It was about mortality; it was to keep his conscious and his memories, then move them from body to body, and then give him the chance to move freely between bodies as…"

Joseph interrupted, "A virus."

Jacob smiled, "Yes, as a virus, but a peaceful one that would never interfere with the body; it would just monitor and report to us in regular meetings."

John asked, "How about Akhenaten's body?"

"Body was never an issue; what matters is the consciousness. Then, with the right technology, we can install this consciousness back on anybody, or even a robot. A few years after this experiment, and as we succeeded in moving his consciousness from body to body, we had to fake Akhenaten's death and then erase all the evidence of our experiments, including his scientists." Jacob replied.

"So, on this double slit experiment, Akhenaten was not the second electron, he was just a camera implanted in this electron, and the electron itself was the human being?" asked Joseph.

"Yes, Joseph, that was Akhenaten's plan for mortality; we had to be patient and not race the time; we had to wait until the 20th century." Jacob replied and then continued, "The experiment worked, and we were able to upload Akhenaten's consciousness, and then we succeeded in giving him full control to move from body to body as we were navigating his movements and giving him gaudiness and in return, we kept your human race memory without interfering. We also promised him we would keep Akhenaten's heir moving to lead countries for better opportunities, as you read in Adam's diary when he moved to London and then to the USA."

The three of them looked at each other before John said, "What do you mean by keeping his heir moving to lead countries as you did with Adam? Are you saying that..."

Jacob looked at Joseph and rushed to say, "Yes, Joseph, you are the last heir of Akhenaten."

Then he continued in a deep voice, making Suzan's body shiver, "And it is all up to you now; you are the one who will decide how this will end."

Joseph was perplexed and scared as John took a defensive position, covering his nephew with his arms, and Suzan looked at Jacob and said, "Don't you ever think you could touch my son."

Jacob remained calm and said, "I am not here to hurt your son; I am here to clear the truth to all of you. I am sure you are all confused, so let me finish what happens, and then we decide the next step."

"For centuries, we've been guiding Akhenaten from body to body. We were excited about the amount of knowledge we learned about your race. Still, we got so excited that we didn't realize the changes occurring within Akhenaten himself until 1889, specifically on May 18th. On that day, Akhenaten, with all his years of knowledge and experience, decided to sit in the driver's seat and choose his host. This host was a newborn baby that the world knew by the name of Thomas Midgley, and he was described in history books as one of the worst inventors who contributed to environmental problems like global warming and many others that eventually led to..." he paused for a moment and said, "end of the world!"

John looked at him in surprise and asked, "Is Thomas Midgley in any way related to Laura?"

"Yes, in this universe, Thomas is Laura's great-grandfather."

He paused briefly, then said, "But in an alternate universe, Laura is Thomas's mother."

They were all surprised, but this was nothing compared to the look in their eyes after Jacob looked at Joseph and pressed his words, "And in that same alternate universe, you are the father."

Jacob paused for a second to give them time to digest all this information. After a few moments passed, he spoke, "But first, let me tell you what happened to this universe since 1889?"

Dilemma

"You can't share this with anyone. Otherwise, everything will change, Jacob. I am not you from an alternate universe; I am you from your future in that same universe, exactly from March 7th, 2025; yes, Jacob, this is the day everything will collapse, so I decided to spend these last few moments with you. Let me correct myself. I didn't decide to send this message; I had to. I had to send it to keep the cycle going; we may have failed or succeeded, but it doesn't matter; what matters is we continue to fulfill this feeling that keeps growing inside you, and you are hiding it from everyone, everyone including yourself, the feeling of power and the thirst of control. It's time to face it, not just face it, but to feel and enjoy it, but that requires patience as it will be a long-term plan, but guess what; we have the time, we have all the time."

"I know you are as confused as I was when I received this message long ago, but if everything is the same, then you're thinking right now: this is a trick, or someone wants to set you up. Also, deep in your thoughts, you wish this is true. It is true, Jacob, and in this message, I will reveal to you the code of the ultimate power in this game."

"Everything you heard with your crew in the first part of the message—is true. Yes, there is a three-dimensional world, and they call it Earth, but only you will call it your kingdom, as on this Earth, you can predict their future and change their past. The only thing you need is to control them, their feelings, thoughts, and their fate; only then will you not be just their king but their God. On this earth, you are immortal as time works differently than in our four-dimensional world, but to be able to do all of that, we will need a plan; we will need to create fear of things that could be true and scary, but only you'll know that it's all under control. We must collect information and create the right tools and technology to achieve our goals. We will need to recruit people from our world, their world, and the multiverse,

160

but without letting them know that they're all working for us, you will act surprised about things you already know because I will tell you everything. You will need to reject offers before accepting them, and in the end, you will need to make tough decisions that may cause you to lose your morals and the one you love the most—but will guarantee you power."

"Not everyone has the strength and the passion to accept this offer, but you will accept it, play this game, and enjoy it. Then, in the end, it could be on the same date or after thousands and thousands of years that you will send the same message back to yourself so you can play again and again. For now, I want you to remember those names as they will be key players in our master plan: Akhenaten, Thomas Midgely, Joseph Jackson, John Carter, Suzan Carter, and David Lee."

"Those are your winning cards, but sometimes, you must eliminate some to win the game. You are smart enough to decide what cards you will keep and which you will sacrifice. Now listen to me carefully, as this part of the message will be encrypted after I am done, so no one can find out until you resend it again."

He kept telling Jacob about the plan and everything that would happen in the future—everything that would turn Jacob from an excellent scientist to God or the devil!

All those thoughts were running through Jacob's mind, remembering the message he received thousands and thousands of years ago. Here, he was getting very close to his goal; he only needed to eliminate the minor obstacles. He smiled and continued…

"Akhenaten kept moving from body to body, and we always guided him where to go and which country would lead the world so he could be there. We always used our prediction of your future and the information from Akhenaten to build an enormous database about your species and learn about you and how you think, feel, and live your life. In the beginning, the data stream was slow, but thanks to our advanced technology team that is working under my supervision, we enhanced the stream and were able to have an accurate prediction about your future and how you will cause the end of this world and all other worlds."

"Akhenaten also learned a lot, and after all those years of knowledge, he became so powerful that he could predict things before we told him about them, and he was always right. By the 18th century, he could move between bodies, alter thoughts and ideas, control feelings, and measure senses. Sometimes, he enters your thoughts and makes you speak his mind."

"Like when Michael visited you on your last piano lesson, he wasn't exactly Michael; he was delivering a message to you from Akhenaten to help you discover the truth."

Joseph repeated to himself, "I was talking to Akhenaten."

Jacob continued, "He was our greatest tool to understand humans. Sometimes, he used these skills for his own benefit, as when he guided your great-grandfather to help discover the tomb, then moved to England and then to the USA, and also when he visited your grandfather in his dreams, taking different shapes, sometimes scary and sometimes peaceful. Until we asked him to get into the body of Thomas Midgley, who was born on May 18th, 1889, and that was our mistake."

"Why?" John asked skeptically.

Jacob answered, "It was our mistake because…"

John interrupted him, "Not why it was your mistake, but why did you ask him to invade the body of a newborn baby?"

"To create the problem would help me control the world." Jacob thought to himself.

But he answered, "Because our data analyses and prediction of the earth's future said that this person will be the direct reason for all the mess that will happen."

John nodded, but he had this feeling that something was not right, so he decided to continue listening to Jacob.

"Thomas grew up to be a genius mechanical engineer. He was climbing up the ladder in his career until the early 1920s when he was working on the problem of a car's engine knocking, and after some research and experiment, he came up with a disastrous solution."

Joseph mumbled, "Leaded gasoline."

"Yes, Joseph, leaded gasoline. That solved the engine knocking but shook the whole future of this world, and by the time they banned it, the damage had happened. Then Midgley didn't stop there; in the 1930s, he invented Freon 12 to be used in refrigerators for cooling, and this gas was one of the direct reasons for Ozone depletion."

"What Midgley did to the world was more destructive than World War I and II combined."

John looked confused and asked, "So the world ended because of Ozone depletion, causing global warming and harmful radiation, but this problem was resolved when we started to monitor the problem and came up with solutions like recycling and Go Green. Besides, Freon was banned a long time ago!"

Jacob nodded his head and said, "Yes and No. Global warming would cause the end of the earth as you know it. Still, your actions helped delay this fate but will not completely stop it, and that is because you still have people in powerful positions and governments who ignore facts and follow their greed, seeking their glory—and that is what ended the world."

Then he looked at Suzan and asked, "Remind us again, what are the side effects of inhaling the leaded gasoline?"

Suzan responded, "Well, between short-term and long-term effects, we are talking about hallucinations, depression, damage to the nervous system, causing a reduced IQ level, and increasing violent crimes."

Joseph shivered as he felt scared from what his mother said, but then Jacob continued asking Suzan, "And what about Freon?"

Suzan put her hands on Joseph's shoulder to calm him down and slowly said, "The central nervous system and the immune system become disruptive."

Jacob then looked at John and said, "Now, what do you expect from a stupid, violent, and sick generation?"

"I expect people like Albert Einstein, Mostafa Mosharafa, and Stephen Hawking. I expect a young generation who sees the problem trying to fix it. I expect hope—I expect anything except giving up."

Jacob looked at him and said, "I agree, but you should also expect FOMO."

Everybody seemed puzzled.

"Fear of Missing Out," said Jacob.

"Because of the people you mentioned, and many others like them, your world jumped great steps and made great leaps on many fields, and because of the promise we made to Akhenaten, we kept your timeline and didn't wipe out your memories, but at the same time, the ignorance, greed, and violence was booming, as you know about the multiverse. Every action will create an altered universe, and those altered decisions will wipe out each other. Only a few will stay—creating the multiverse. But with all the technology, your species starts to build the fear of missing out; you want to try everything, and you start to jump from one decision to another without a clear goal or clear vision; you start talking a lot and acting less, you start to question everything and anything, and then lose track. You start trying to reinvent the wheel, and all these decisions create different universes to create other universes, eventually leading to a space traffic jam, the whole space-time will collapse… it will be the… something your culture knew as…"

"Doomsday." He completed the sentence after a pause.

Joseph looked very nervous and asked Jacob, "In 1940, Thomas Midgley got infected by Polio and died in 1944 because of asphyxiation when he was trying one of his inventions; it is not common that someone gets polio at that late age, was that you behind his death?"

Jacob looked at him with a smile and said, "Did you just google this information?"

Joseph smiled, "I don't need to google it, Jacob; after thousands of years, Google would be my last name."

"And your first name would be Akhenaten, finally, my old friend," said Jacob.

Without saying a word, and before anyone could react, Joseph jumped in the air, made a backflip to grab the kitchen knife, and rotated it. The knife stopped in the air, and the shape of the statue started to shape around the knife, with blood dropping on the floor as the knife was right at the statue's heart. Joseph jumped right in front of the statue and pushed the knife into the heart. As the statue's eyes went wide open and blood came out from its mouth, it started to take the form of a human. Joseph looked straight into his eyes and said, "This is your payback for all the people you killed, Terry, Laura, David, and many others, and by the way, we are not primitive."

The statue dropped dead on the floor with a complete formation to human shape. John looked at the body on the floor and mumbled, "Oh my God, this is Peter."

Suzan was still caught by surprise and couldn't say anything as she dropped on her chair. After all that happened, Jacob was still sitting very calmly with the same smile on his face!

Joseph looked at him and said, "I bet you didn't see this coming, Jacob."

Jacob looked at him and leaned forward, "There is nothing I don't see coming; I am sure you knew that!"

Suzan was still shocked and looked at Joseph, "Who are you? You are not my son!"

Joseph put his hand on his mom's shoulder and said, "You're right, but don't worry, I'm just trying to finish what I should have done many years ago; Joseph is safe."

Then he looked at Jacob and said, "Now I think it is time to tell the truth, Jacob. It's time to tell them what you have done and why you did it."

John was still looking at Peter's body. "How did you know he was standing there, and how did you kill him?"

Joseph smiled, "Try to live five thousand years with all the knowledge and experience, and you will be able to do things you never thought possible. Peter was here from the beginning to kill me as they tried to kill me when I was in Thomas's body, but to kill me, he had to transform into a human shape, so I just aimed the knife with the right speed at the right moment."

"But why did they want to kill you? I thought you guys were teamed up!" Suzan asked.

Joseph looked at his mom, pointed towards Jacob, and said, "Because I knew that everything he told you was a twisted fact to reach his goal." Then he looked at Jacob and said, "Do you know who else knows that?"

Jacob was getting ready to kill him and finish the job, but then he paused and listened.

Message

Sarah was in the lab looking at the screen in front of her and trying different codes to break this strange message they had received years ago. While fully concentrating on cracking the code, she didn't notice that her other screen showed a folder uploading, but then she heard that ding sound of receiving an email. She was surprised when she found that she'd sent that email to herself, and what caught her eyes was the subject; "Akhenaten and Nefertiti, please read alone."

She was alone in her private room at the lab but looked around to ensure no one else was there. She closed the door and returned to her computer to see the message.

She clicked on the message. It was a video; she was surprised when she saw herself beside someone. The video started with Sarah saying, "Hi Sarah, before you think this is a trick, let me tell you that this is you, but from an altered universe, and the one next to me is someone you will meet several years from now. His name is Akhenaten, but he will look different as he is hosted in another body; that body for a person will be known as Nikola Tesla."

Sarah felt suspicious about this weird message with such nonsense. Sarah continued watching, "If everything works as planned timewise, then someone will knock at the door now and will ask you if there is any progress on breaking the code of the encrypted message, and you will say we are getting there, and he will reply, I can't wait to tell Dr. Jacob about the results and see his face reaction, and you will reply, that you bet, your dad will not have any reaction, and he will say, deal!"

Right after that part of the video, she hears a knock at the door, and Sarah finds herself saying the same thing as if she were reading some script.

She played the video again, and Sarah in the video said, "OK, now I hope you have started to trust what you are seeing in this video. I will give you the right algorithm to break the code so you can see the message you received years ago, but there will be another part of this message. I want you to watch it, but don't tell anyone about it; you mustn't tell anyone about what you will watch. Otherwise, you will be risking everyone's existence."

The video explained how to break the code, and Sarah took notes and then decoded the message. She found her father on the screen. She carefully listened to everything he said and was astonished by the amount of information until she reached the part where Jacob asked everyone to leave the room. She continued watching, with tears filling her eyes as she couldn't believe that her father would turn into that monster, killing people and destroying universes just for the sake of power.

She completed the video with a broken heart of sadness and frustration, and then she played the other video to see herself talking again, "If you already broke the code, then I know how you feel. I was devastated when I watched this video years ago, but it is up to you to change this fate. Some universes ignored this message and ended up either vanishing or under the control of the heartless law that your dad will establish. Let me show you what would happen if you didn't carefully listen to everything I asked you to do."

The video paused, and another video popped up. It was a video of John sitting at his desk typing on his computer with a gun next to him; the date on the video showed the year 2035. After a few seconds, John stopped typing and held the Gun close to his heart before he pulled the trigger and dropped dead. The video stopped, and another video popped up.

In the video, Sarah said, "I'm sorry you had to watch that, but this is the fate of the people in one of the universes where you ignored my message. The man you saw in this video is not just any man; he is the man you will love, and if things go in the right direction, he might be your husband in the future, and when I say future, I mean the very far future."

Sarah was sobbing and trying to calm down while listening to herself in the video.

"Now, it is crucial and imperative that you do not share this information with anyone, especially Akhenaten, until he is hosted in Nicola Tesla's body. If you told him anything or shared this video with anyone, then the streamlining of incidents will change and create an alternate universe that will move in different routes that could change your current universe into unpredictable patterns. You will need to follow your father's leads on everything but secretly, and after you share the truth with Akhenaten, you will work together on defeating your dad's plan to stop him from ruling the world and eventually causing doomsday."

The video paused for a second and then continued…

"Your Dad plans to convince all of you that because of a human named Thomas Midgely, the universes will begin to collapse, what will be known as FOMO, but what happens is that people on earth start paying attention to the cure when they face the disease, this is the nature of human beings; every once a while they need a wake-up call."

Sarah paused the video and asked, "Earth? Human beings? What is Earth?"

She shrugged her shoulders and played the video again. Only then did she lift her eyebrows, astonished as the video said, "Earth is a three-dimensional world, a place you will choose in the future to live in, where you will have a husband and children. Human beings are creatures that live on earth. Now, I need you to listen carefully to what we ask you to do."

A man in the video said, "Sarah, please keep this message with you all the time, and at the right moment, you will show it to me, not before and not after. Read the exact date on the video; you will know where to find me by then. Now, I will tell you how we will stop your dad from destroying the whole world. Together, we will stop doomsday, or at least we'll stop your dad from causing it."

Control

When Sarah knocked on the door, Jacob was sitting in his office reviewing the data downloaded from Akhenaten and was consumed with analyzing graphs and numbers.

"Come in, Sarah."

Sarah walked in and asked her dad, "How did you know that was me at the door?"

He looked at her and said, "Sarah, you are the only polite person in this building who still knocks and waits for an answer….no one else does that. Also, I can see you in this camera."

Sarah shook her head to clear her thoughts before she looked at her dad. In a serious tone, she said, "We need Akhenaten on a special mission."

Jacob crossed his fingers in front of his face and looked straight into Sarah's eyes. He then leaned forward and, in his calm voice, said, "Who are we? And what mission?"

Sarah felt that her dad's eyes were digging into her brain and reading her thoughts, but she put her thoughts together and tried to be as calm as possible. "We are the research team. If Akhenaten succeeds in this mission, we will save ourselves a lot of work and be able to travel between the multiverse without causing any disturbance in the timestream."

Sarah felt nervous, as she decided to tell Jacob her true intentions and only hide the small details. She wanted to safely send the message to the multiverse as she had received it. This loop must continue and never be interrupted if she wants to save the universe from the ultimate end.

When Jacob heard the idea of traveling between the multiverse, he was filled with excitement. He tried to hide his enthusiasm and asked Sarah to keep talking.

Sarah noticed her father's eagerness and continued, "Nikola Tesla." She paused for a moment to see her father's expression. Then continued, "This scientist will do a lot of research about energy, and with this research, we will be able to break the borders between the multiverse and communicate with our peers.

Jacob looked at her and said, "But we are already communicating with the multiverse, so how will this research benefit us?"

Sarah quickly said, "We communicate with them only when they decide to communicate, and it only happens when they wish it to happen. Besides, we don't know the exact tools they use when communicating. Maybe what they are doing is affecting our timestream in a way we will never know; perhaps what is happening was not supposed to happen the same way, but it only happened because of these regular meetings in our universe!"

Her Dad seemed pretty convinced. Sarah continued, "This research, with the help of our technology, allows us to gain control and be more powerful. If you notice, there's nothing to lose; it'll be a quick mission for Akhenaten, and then we can send him back into Thomas Midgley."

Jacob paused for a second before nodding his head. "OK, I will communicate with him and give him the coordinates and…"

Sarah interrupted him, "I will go by myself."

"You miss him?" Jacob asked.

"Yes," she answered quickly, leaving the office. Before stepping out, she turned back and went around the office to hug her dad. She held his face and said, "I love you, Dad." With that, she left the office without looking back; she said, "It will be a quick trip; it is for all of us," then she mumbled, "It is to save all of us."

Jacob kept looking at her till she left the office. He felt a little emotional with her hug, but then he went back to the data on his disk and smiled, saying, "More power and more control, hell! why not!"

He opened another file and started checking some drawings and numbers. He whispered to himself, "I think it is time to replace you, Akhenaten, with something that is not asking questions or discussing orders, something Sarah will never fall in love with, something that could be a cure and death at the same time for this race!"

He said it while checking a sketch of a drone, the same drone that years from now, our world will call a deadly virus!

Death

Jacob was listening to Joseph as he figured out that his only daughter was tricking him since the beginning, and all his plans were already exposed before they even began, but then the concern on his face started to turn into a smile, and the smile turned into laughter that made both Suzan and John look at each other in wonder. Joseph kept his eyes on Jacob, and Joseph tried to interrupt the laugh, "Looks like you are entertained by all these facts; let me entertain you more and tell you what happened."

"No need, Joseph. I can see what happens next; let me continue the story for you." He sat straight with his eyes focused on Joseph before he started to talk.

"Sarah sent the new coordinates to you, Akhenaten, and when you invaded Nicola Tesla's body, she arranged a meeting with you, and then during that meeting, she showed you the message to convince you to help her send the same message to all alternate universes, and you did it as Nicole Tesla. With all your knowledge about power and energy, you were able to open secure gates between universes, and not only that, but your research was also the beginning of time travel. Do you see what you and Sarah did here? Because of you, I received the message from me in the future. You tried to solve a problem you created from the beginning. Yes, Akhenaten, your interference with time was why I turned into what I am now, and it was the reason that ended the world and caused doomsday. Those traffic jams that I told you about would never have happened even with the infinity universes as long as they didn't interact, but you opened the gates, causing the creation of many other universes that were never supposed to interact or exist; they were suddenly able to see each other which distorted memories, causing fear and panic for no reason, and then, this effect was increased by the FOMO, and out of nowhere, we came in the middle of this vicious circle. That is why I had to interact, take control, and save what I could."

John interrupted with sarcasm in his voice, "That is the excuse that every dictator uses to justify their actions."

He continued, "You didn't want to control the world to save it; you wanted it because that was your dream, passion, and desire that you hid from everyone else, even yourself. This message you received didn't change you to be what you are now; it was just revealing the cover to show exactly what you are all the time. This message was the Quiz, your quiz, Jacob, the quiz that we all receive at a certain point in our life, and we either pass it or we break and fall into the trap, and then we call it 'fate' and keep telling ourselves that it is meant to be! As Carl Jung aptly said, *'Unless you bring the unconscious into conscious, it'll direct your life, and you will call it fate.'* The quiz was not for us; it was for you, and you broke down and failed."

"What about you, John? Did you pass your quiz, or did you also break down?"

Before John answered, Joseph looked at Jacob and asked, "Then, Dr. Jacob, what did you do to take control?"

"To control and rule, I had to create fear, then with the fear you create hope and the cure, until everyone in your world and my world believes that I am the cure, and I am the hope. So, first, we created the virus from day one, as you know, that helped your race brainstorm and evolve. No dictator wants to rule primitives; you need to have some knowledge and some ethics, but only to a certain point, and both of these originate from a crisis; then it is time for phase two, which is collecting data and fully control your race, so we had to create what would look like a virus, but at the same time we could control it, and decide who is to keep serving us, and who is useless and should be eliminated."

Then he looked at Suzan and said, "Killing David was not my call, but I wouldn't do anything different. David was supposed to work on finding a cure to the virus, but his research moved on a different route, and we had to stop him; then we had to take out Terry to create the balance and open a door for a replacement on the research route to create what we would call *the cure.*"

Suzan looked at him with eyes full of hate and said, "What cure, and who is the replacement?"

"The cure that you will invent, Dr. Suzan."

He smiled at Suzan's expression and continued, "After we created fear and had full control, and as everyone is scared and ready to accept any sacrifice to live a normal life, there would be a third phase."

He paused to look at Suzan and continued viciously, "The cure…"

Akhenaten inside Joseph interrupted, "The cure that will make him gain full control, turning this world into big concentration camps, where people would live, work and play, but all under his supervision, and whenever someone turns forty, he grants him wishes for twenty-four hours, before either the person kills himself, or the drones inside him will finish their job."

Jacob looked at him and continued, "Yes, and that will take us to the fourth and most important phase—taking down whoever's knowledge passes a certain level, some ripples and oppositions are accepted; it is requisites to guarantee the full control of the mass, but when someone's knowledge passes a certain level, then this person must be eliminated, and who has more knowledge than you, Akhenaten? After all these thousands of years living among the finest human beings and learning from your world and our world, that is why you had to go, and your existence became a glitch in my perfect system, a glitch that I had to fix."

"That is why you tried to kill Thomas Midgley, using polio?" Akhenaten asked.

Jacob sounded angry, "Yes, but you never came back from Tesla's body, and we lost track; even with our drones in every human being, we couldn't find you, so we had to go back to the beginning, and I was sure you would end up here in Joseph's body, your last offspring."

"Where do you think we will go after the truth has been revealed and your only daughter knows about your plan?" John asked.

Jacob checked his watch, then said, "First, I will do this…" he clicked a button on his watch, then said, "This is the exact moment and place to send the same message to myself in the past. However, I added a few details to prepare me for my daughter's betrayal." He continued looking at Joseph, "Then, I will need to find another assistant after you killed my loyal scientist."

Then, Jacob looked at John and said, "Peter, as you knew him, was working at Facts and watching you and Terry closely."

Then his face turned to be mad looking at Joseph. He said, "Finally, after some calculations, I found that Suzan and John knew too much, and you know what that means."

As soon as he finished the sentence, John and Suzan's faces turned red—the drones started to attack them. While they were struggling with death, Jacob looked at Joseph and said, "What you are missing is that the drones inside Joseph's body are designed in a special way to track Akhenaten's DNA."

He paused and then turned and spoke in a killer's tone, "I love being in this human body shape; it makes me enjoy the feelings of anger and love, but the best of all—revenge."

"Don't worry, Joseph, I might save your life, but first, I need to kill the devil inside you."

At that moment, he gave the order to the drones inside Joseph's body to attack Akhenaten.

Joseph's face turned red; he fell on his knees and covered his face with his hands.

The Beginning

Tesla was writing equations on his notes, then slowly started to draw an infinity sign and kept tracing his pen over and over on the sign before looking at Sarah. He said, "After you trace this sign many times, you lose track, and you won't be able to tell where the starting and end points were. Do you even remember how all of this began?"

Sarah looked at him and said, "Who am I talking to now? Is that you, Akhenaten, or am I talking to Nicola Tesla?"

Tesla smiled before his smile turned into laughter. He said, "Even though I lost track of it, in the beginning, I was able to control the body, the mind, and the soul while keeping the person's identity and letting them live their life normally, but then, I started to lose the boundaries. Sometimes, I feel they are the ones who are within me and not vice versa; it is more like two people in a car, both holding the wheel. If they didn't work together, they would crash the car."

His voice became cheerful, and he said, "But so far, no accidents, and to answer your question, it is me." With that, he stood up and walked towards her. She stood up, too. He came closer, touched her chin with his fingers, and gently kissed her lips.

She whispered in a voice full of love, "Akhenaten."

Then she cleared her throat and moved her hands on her hair to calm herself down before she moved around the room at Tesla's house and said, "Yes, sometimes the beginning happens after the end, or within the same moment, or before. It all depends on which universe we are talking about."

He shook his head and said, "Only now I understand when you asked me to visit John Wallis to motivate him with all the knowledge I gained over thousands of years to develop a mathematical infinity sign, but I am still confused because years after that, you will meet

Tesla, who would help you to deliver messages over multiverse and through time as well, the same messages that let you know that we existed as human beings millions of years ago!"

She nodded in agreement and said in a sad voice, "Yes, the same message that turned my dad into what he is now…" then she paused briefly and continued, "…or what will he be in a different time and altered universe?"

He looked at her as he remembered something and said, "Yes, speaking about your dad, what are you going to do with his DNA sample?"

Sarah looked at him as she remembered the message she had received from herself in an altered universe.

"Sarah, when you meet Jacob, I want you to get a sample of his DNA; act like you're gently hugging and touching his face. Your nails should carry some of his DNA. You will need this sample to swap it with another and make it look like a sample from people on Earth. There will be a scientist who will help you with this, but she should never know your identity or why you're doing that. You will contact this scientist through secure communication, then take the results, and you will know what to do with them at the right time. This scientist's name is Suzan Garner."

***

Joseph's face was completely red, and he covered it before he cracked laughing too loud—Jacob was looking at him with a face full of surprise. He started to feel the poking in his throat, and his body temperature started rising. He couldn't understand what was happening to him.

Joseph looked at him and said, "Remember when the last time Sarah hugged you was to take your DNA? Then, years and years after that, we deceived your virus and replaced my DNA with yours, and here you are, killing yourself and tasting the feeling of death as you caused it to millions of people. You were right; being in a human's body makes you have all these feelings of hate, love, revenge, and, best of all—death. As you are trapped in this agony, I let you send the message as I will enjoy playing the same game with you on a different level, but no matter how many times we play, every time, I will enjoy looking at you—dying in pain, and every time I look at your burning eyes; I say—Game Over."

Jacob's eyes were turning red as if he was on fire. He remembered how his daughter tricked him, but even though he was pained, he still felt proud of his daughter's smartness.

His smile quickly disappeared with a big scream, as blood started to pour out of his eyes and mouth, and he dropped dead in his blood. His body slowly began to turn into an undefined shape before vanishing.

Joseph looked at him with a smile that appeared more than five thousand years old.

He gasped as Akhenaten left his body, and Joseph dropped to the floor subconsciously, but his mind was screaming, "John, Suzan, Terry, Laura, David!"

Next Level

Los Angeles - California

Monday, March 19, 2021

10:10 AM

"John, Suzan, Terry, Laura, David!"

A scream was coming out of the room as a group of nurses and doctors were trying to control what seemed like a case of agitation before the body on the bed completely collapsed, and one of the doctors said, "We are losing him; his vitals are unstable."

Another doctor started injecting medication, "He is stable now; all vitals are okay," he said, walking outside the room to his office with the other doctor. He looked at the nurse and said, "Keep an eye on him, and when he wakes up, you can take him to the garden."

The nurse nodded, and the two doctors walked towards the office with the sign, 'Dr. Ed Jacob, Head of Mental Health Department.'

The other Doctor looked at Dr. Jacob and said, "This case is unique, but I admire your treatment plan; even with him collapsing today, the amount of data we got out of his brain is enormous, and it will help with many similar cases."

Jacob smiled as he leaned forward toward his computer's monitor and clicked on a file named Joseph Garner. "I can't claim that credit for myself. I have been dealing with Joseph's case for six months now, and he was already suffering from minor signs of autism. A young man, who is 25 years old, is working in a café called Facts, living with his sister and her husband, as the three of them work in the same café. He also has a girlfriend about to get her degree in psychology; his life was quite happy and stable, and he was managing his day between working and reading history books, especially Egyptology, and studying online programs to be a journalist. Everything was smooth until Covid hit his family—he lost both his sister and his girlfriend within the same month. But the real tragedy happened when he lost his brother-in-law."

"You mean Terry?"

"Yes, remember the demonstrations of May 2020 with regards to the brutal death of Floyd? During these demonstrations, Terry was killed, and that was the breakdown for Joseph. When he arrived here, he was in complete denial. It was a phase where he kept mentioning different names, some of whom we knew as his family. Then he added other names of the people dealing with him in the last few months, for instance, me and Peter, his nurse, Fatima and Isaac, who are patients in the institution. But then he started to make up characters, like David, for example, and then replaced himself with another person and named him John Carter, as John was everything Joseph wanted to be."

He stopped talking as someone was knocking on the door. A nurse walked in and said, "Joseph is going to the backyard with his book and notes."

Jacob thanked the nurse and looked from his window to see Joseph sitting, wearing his shades and holding his book.

"Dr. Jacob, may I come in?" a voice came from the door.

Jacob turned and, with a big smile, asked the guest to sit down as he looked towards the other doctor and said, "As I was saying, I can't take the whole credit for myself because she was the one who got the idea that helped us to find the treatment plan," he said pointing to the guest!

The other doctor nodded and said, "Nice to meet you."

Jacob smiled and continued, "The idea was to put Joseph in the same world he created for himself, so we started to listen carefully to all his comments, encouraging him to write notes and only calling him by the name he chose for himself until it was the right moment; we put him in a simulator program, that matched everything he dreamed about. There was only one issue, and that was the key to the treatment!"

The other doctor said, "The coffee."

Jacob and his guest nodded as he continued, "Part of his mind was refusing this artificial world and wanted to remind Joseph about his true identity, and the coffee was the exit, as that was his job and his real senses were smelling, seeing and touching the coffee all day long, but he kept resisting this feeling as he altered everything around him to stay in a comfort zone. So, he started to see me as the bad guy; the patients with him were the ones helping him. Terry and Laura betrayed him so he wouldn't feel the agony of losing them, but at the same time, he gave himself an exit as they betrayed him in an altered universe. He even resisted and refused the idea that Laura was his girlfriend. Then his sister, who always took care of him, was his mom in the world he created, as he tried to place himself as Joseph but as a 10-year-old so he could have hope and peace of mind, but..."

He paused.

This time, the guest asked, "But what, Dr. Jacob?"

"Sarah, Joseph never met you, so how come he used your name as the main character in his story? Not just that, he even described you exactly as you are!"

Sarah moved her hair behind her ears, looked at Jacob with a charming smile, and said, "I wish I had an answer. This case can use everything around him to make it part of the story, so he might have heard you mention my name."

Then she winked her eyes with laughter and said, "Also, he might've heard you describing how I look."

She laughed loudly, waving her hands, saying, "I'm sure that is not the case; he may have seen me when I was visiting your office and walking through the garden."

Dr. Jacob nodded his head as he accepted the last explanation. Sarah stood up and said, "As we have successfully gotten all his thoughts out of his mind and we let his reality deal with his imagination, I think we are ready for the second phase of treatment, and that will be by making him meet the real people he imagined and introduce them to him. I should start by myself."

With that, she stood up and started walking towards the door.

Dr. Jacob said, "Do you think I should be with you when you meet him for the first time?"

"No, I think that will be too much for him; you and I were the main characters in his story, so let's take it one at a time."

Jacob nodded, but the other doctor said before Sarah left the office, "What if all that was not just hallucinations?"

Sarah stopped and turned, "What do you mean?"

He took a deep breath and said, "What if there is actually a metaverse? What if Joseph in this universe is John in another universe? And what if everything he imagined was not his imagination but memories of the same person in another universe? Think about it; he mentioned in the book when he talked about the Mandela effect!"

Sarah walked back till she was a few inches from the other doctor. She asked, "I am sorry, but I never got your name?"

Dr. Jacob said, "Sorry, this is my fault. I didn't introduce you to each other; as you know, this is Dr. Sarah Adam, and she's handling

Joseph's case with me. And this is Dr. Michael Mina; he's the intern from Egypt and just joined us a month ago."

"Hello, Michael. I'm pleased to meet you. Egypt is a fascinating country." Sarah had a mysterious smile on her lips.

Michael smiled back and said, "It is for sure."

Sarah nodded and turned to leave the office. At the door, she turned back, looking at Michael. She said, "So, if that was not a story, and it was, as you said, a slipping memory from an altered universe, then we only have four years before Armageddon."

She paused for a second to make sure they got scared. She laughed and said, "You should see your faces now!"

She continued, "But it is just a story from a case with a disturbed mind that denies reality because of an unfortunate series of events—a story that could be a bestselling book!"

She said that and left the office, leaving Michael and Jacob looking at each other, thinking; what if…

Sitting on his garden chair, Joseph was reading his book when Sarah approached him and said, "Hello."

Joseph lifted his head, looking at Sarah. She smiled and said, "I missed you."

Then she began to fade right before Joseph's eyes, while simultaneously, he heard the giggling sounds of children. He could smell the strong coffee, and Sarah completely faded out.

***

He took off his shades to find himself sitting on his couch in his living room as Sarah stood in front of him with a mug of coffee, saying, "It has been hours, Joseph!"

He smiled and said, "Yes, I must rest before starting the next level."

"Did you decide the name or not?" Sarah asked.

He looked away and said, "So far… it is The Quiz!"

With that said, he stood and walked with her to the backyard where their children, Isaac and Fatima, were playing. He put his shades on the table, and on the side of the shades, you could see a familiar sign that looked like a lazy eight. Or was it… infinity…

THE END